Whistle

ALSO BY JANICE DAUGHARTY

Novels

Earl in the Yellow Shirt
Pawpaw Patch
Necessary Lies
Dark of the Moon

Stories

Going Through the Change

Whistle

A Novel

JANICE DAUGHARTY

HarperFlamingo
An Imprint of HarperCollinsPublishers

For Teford Sullivan

HarperCollins books may be purchased for educational, business, or sales promotional use. For information please write: Special Markets Department, HarperCollins Publishers, Inc., 10 East 53rd Street, New York, NY 10022.

FIRST EDITION

Designed by Elina D. Nudelman

Library of Congress Cataloging-in-Publication Data

Daugharty, Janice, 1944–
    Whistle : a novel / Janice Daugharty. —1st ed.
        p.   cm.
    ISBN 0-06-017551-6
    I. Title.
    PS3554.A844W48   1998
    813'.54—dc21   97-42166
                                                                    CIP

98 99 00 01 02 ❖/RRD 10 9 8 7 6 5 4 3 2

ACKNOWLEDGMENTS

Much thanks to Aberjhani, one of my favorite poets,
whose experiences inspired a good deal of this story; and
to Dr. Anthony Clark at the State Crime Lab in Moultrie,
Georgia, whose expertise kept this story on track. Thanks
also to Seward, my detail man, and to Jason Kaufman,
Ginger Barber, Cornelius Howland, and Larry Ashmead
for turning this manuscript into a book.

BOOK ONE **Roper**

1

Roper hopes he isn't seeing what he thinks he's seeing, but he is, he knows he is. He hopes it's a roll of navy rags tumbled up by the wind that isn't wind but a drizzly draft batting through the truck window. Eyes on the roll of navy at the end of the pond road, he steers the blue Isuzu onto the rough ground of the open field, driving north toward the blue tractor, to get on with his mowing. Watching till the strand of unmowed weeds blocks his view of the navy rag roll. When he looks again, it will be gone. Surely it will be gone.

But when he mounts the tractor and gears it into first, looking again toward the end of the pond road, he is high enough to see over the weeds and still the roll of navy is there. Not exactly a roll shape, and if he isn't careful he might conjure the rest of it into the image of a white woman's overlapped arms and legs. Driving parallel to the navy and white—what? rags blown from the old homesite on the south end of the property?—yet a good hundred feet away, he heads the tractor east in the direction of the white farmhouse fronting Highway 129, listening to the hard *chirr* of the rotary mower, the mind-numbing *clata-clat-clat* of the tractor. Seeing before him the green Volvo in the backyard where he'd talked to the boss's wife before going home for lunch. Wearing what? One of those shorts outfits she wears when she goes out walking every day. What color? He can lie to himself and say red or gray. He can lie to himself and say he never spoke to that white woman in the first place, that he hasn't seen what could be her body sideslung in the sand at the other end of the road.

But he has.

In the pecan orchard, field side of the rail-fenced yard, he turns the tractor, mowing west into the fuzzy brown weeds and grasshopper flurries, eyes on the navy roll that he tries to fool himself into believing has moved. Maybe she is resting. Maybe she is trying to lure Roper into coming to check on her; maybe Math Taylor has told his wife to test Roper. But knowing Taylor, whom Roper has worked either with or for, off and on, since the early part of his fifty-four years when he became workable, Roper knows that isn't right. That Math Taylor would do his own testing if he wanted to test somebody. Two weeks Roper's been working for Taylor, this time, and two weeks he's been trying not to look at the white woman, who could land his ass back in jail. Not that she's been anything but kind to him, too kind.

Getting closer to the navy and white hump, Roper decides to really look this time. Almost level with it, though still maybe ninety feet to his left, he can see her gray-blond hair cooped over her left arm. Right arm covering her face as if she is playing peekaboo with a baby. But the right toe of her white running shoe is flexed inward in a way that this lady would never flex her foot, maybe even if she was dead. Dead, she has to be dead. Did she have a heart attack, did somebody murder her, did a rattlesnake bite her? Maybe a stray shot from a deer hunter's rifle.

All the way up to the row of pine saplings circling the pond, so close Roper can see the shrunken black water, and again he turns the tractor, juddering it over the furrows of dirt and wintering weeds, toward the house again, past the woman again, now some seventy-five feet away. Watching behind him the body and letting the tractor cruise randomly through ragweeds and dog fennels, goatspur and blackberry thickets. When he has to look ahead again, when he has to steer the tractor into the neat etched line of sagy cured weeds on his right, away from the pale green stubble on his left, that clean patch every day for two weeks the tractor has been gnawing away at, his hands are shaking so badly he has to grind them into the steering wheel. To make them stick.

Next run, and the drizzle changes to rain. A slow slanting rain across the same impossible but peaceful two hundred acres he's been whittling away at for two weeks—he's never worked so steady for so long before. The field peaceful now except for the navy roll that hasn't moved. Same down-flexed right shoe and right arm over the face. Hell, even Sweet, the quarters' whore, crazy as she is, wouldn't lie down to rest in the rain! In the middle of a weed field?

When it rains, generally, Roper can go home and sleep or wander the quarters, a mile south of Taylor's place. He should go now, a good excuse. Passing the parked pickup on his left and the roll of navy on his right, he is tempted to stop, to get into the truck, to go home, but instead makes a quick right. Straight across the humpy field, stopping the tractor a few weed-choked furrows away from the body or whatever.

Rain streams down his hot face—so hot this last day of

October! He calls out, "Hey, hey! Hey, Miss Lora! Hey!" The word "hey" feels stuck in his throat, and doesn't sound proper anyway when addressing the white woman. Does it matter? "Hey, get up," he yells through the muffler of rain. "You awright?"

Rain spots spread on her navy shorts and shirt, the toe of her right shoe still points down. No blood that he can see. He is so close he can make out the heel stitching of her white sock showing above the back of her shoe, the untied shoelace—a bad sign—and realizes he is walking toward her, whistling, rather than standing in one spot as he'd thought. Rain beating straight down on his cap now, straight down on the woman's gray-blond hair. So strange in the sandy dirt.

Still whistling, he wheels and starts toward the idling blue tractor; not blue, like navy, but what a woman might call bright blue, what his mama, loving color, might call royal blue. The old tractor bluer than normal with the rain rinsing the cottony fuzz of weeds from the bent left fender. Not Roper's fault, the bent fender. Nobody can blame him for the bent fender. Nobody has tried to. Will they blame him for the white woman's death or whatever? Probably. He stops whistling, starts to moan.

Walking past the idling tractor, toward the pickup, blue too, though more sky blue, he peers up into the rain at the sky that is boggy-mud gray instead of blue. He has to keep staring at some blank space like that till he can get the hell out of this field. He has to go. He will tell Math Taylor that he didn't come back after lunch—raining, you know. Bossman will like that; won't have to pay whatever part of twenty-five dollars for a half day he would have to pay if Roper had come back.

In the truck, Roper grabs his brown plaid flannel over-shirt and wipes the rain from his face. Starting the truck fast and driving it fast, due east through the mowed part of the field. In the pecan orchard, he stops and peers back through the scrim of rain, and for a minute fools himself into believing that the navy roll is gone, that the woman is gone, that the woman was never there in the first place. Following the truck path around the first pecan tree, around the second pecan tree, past the tin equipment shed on his right, through the gap in the rail fence and past the live oak in the sideyard, he stares at the tall white house where he can see what he imagines is the kitchen light through the window. Yes, the kitchen. Roper saw it through the front double window last week while he was sweeping down cobwebs from the front porch, which he had hated doing with the boss gone because you never can tell what a white woman might say or do. What she'd said was "Roper, that looks good," when he'd finished, but had reset the porch rockers on the porch he is now passing. An edgy woman, just shy of fifty, the kind who can't be still and who, in this case, is afraid she'll seem afraid of a black man simply because he is black, but whose fear shows anyway.

Up the sandy lane to the highway, and Roper has to wait for a white dump truck to pass, terrified that the driver might know Math Taylor and might tell when his wife's body is found that he, the driver, has seen Roper-the-doper leaving after noon rather than before. In the rain. Terrified that the driver of the dump truck, speed-ing past the house with great tires spuming water, might have seen Lora Taylor lying at the end of the pond road that even Roper himself cannot see, sitting still and star-ing in the rearview mirror.

Turning around, heading back along the south side of the house, around the pecan trees, up the pond road, he tells himself that he is just looking one more time—just one more time—and tells himself too that he is as sorry and crazy as his mama claims—every day since he got out of jail, two months ago, for trafficking in crack cocaine—and tells himself he'll never go back to jail, that this woman sideslung in the dirt up the road, blurry through the rain, is nothing to him.

Out of the truck again and standing in the rain again, he yells, "Hey, you awright? Hey, what . . . what you doing there?" Hanging to the truck door and gawking, shaking, getting drenched. Then letting go of the door and stepping closer, close, till he can hear the ticking of rain turn to splatting on her body. He can hear the *clata-clat-clat* of the idling tractor he has forgotten to switch off. Damn!

"Miss Lora, I come to see if . . ." He stops, feeling the words sop up in the rain. Mumbling on his way back to the truck, "Ain't nothing to me," looking behind to see if she has heard with her arm over one ear and the other ear stuck to the dirt as if she is listening to the sand filtering raindrops. A smart woman, always doing stuff around the yard—looking at birds, looking at leaves drifting down from the trees—she might do that. He tries to recall all he has heard about the woman, which amounts to what he's only half-heard from his mama, because he always half-listens. Lora Taylor is from Somewhere Else. A good enough explanation.

❖ ❖ ❖

This time, Roper stops at the highway in front of the Taylor house, and a black man whose name Roper can't remember, but who he remembers having sold some crack cocaine once, passes on the wet highway in an old rust-brown Pontiac, and waves. Roper scooches low, waves. He isn't supposed to be driving since he got out of jail—probation officer said he better not—has told Taylor that, but Taylor said, "If you get caught driving from the quarters to my place, I'll bail you out of jail," because Roper's driving is convenient for Taylor. Though that's not it altogether, either; truth is, Taylor has created a job so that Roper can pay off his fine: thirty-five hundred dollars, installments of seventy-five dollars a month. Roper waits for the rust car to vanish down the highway in the rain, for the truck's windshield wipers to lay waste to the singing of the car tires on gravel.

His heart starts aching like a pulled muscle. He has been seen. Now two people know he has come back to work this afternoon. He has to get rid of the body, or go home and call somebody, though he has no idea who. Taylor, if Roper can figure where to find him. Working somewhere on one of his construction sites in Valdosta. Roper doesn't know where and doesn't really care because Taylor not putting him to work on a real job means Taylor doesn't think he is capable. But Roper does know that by sundown he might very well end up back in jail, he might be back with the other jailbirds cussing and shoving—that hellhole—and rowdy as Roper has been in the past, he just doesn't have the heart for such anymore.

On his way through the field this time, he is pleased that the rain hasn't let up, that it has almost covered his tire tracks. But what difference? He is putting down more tracks, he is crazy; yes, he is going back. But as he sees that water is puddling around the woman's short, stocky body, he knows he is doing the right thing, that he cannot leave the wife of the man who once saved his life lying there in the rain. And what if she's had a heart attack and isn't dead yet?

Time to touch her. No more crazy talk. Maybe just touch her with the toe of his boot. But if she isn't dead, maybe just passed out, and comes to with the toe of his boot moving the arm over her face, what will she think? What will she tell Taylor, who thirty years ago had rescued Roper from a mob torturing him because he might be *thinking* about touching a white women?

Roper reaches down and lifts her cold right arm, exposing her parted blue lips. Letting the arm fall away and twist her body so that the dry chest of her navy shirt, her flattened breasts, receive the rain, her slit eyes brim with rain like tears.

"Hey," he says again. Backing up. "Hey, Miss Lora, you awright? I ain't getting into this, I ain't getting into this." Saying it while he scoops up her solid body and cradles her to the truck, stuffing her into the cab, where the rain pecks peacefully on the roof. She curls over on the seat with her legs on the floor, almost kneeling. He has to shove at her rounded rump to make room for himself to get inside and drive across the south end of the field, past the old homesite where, pilfering, he has seen a pile of navy rags, and on toward the woodsy nook and the creek where the deer guts he'd dumped for Taylor that morning are bobbing and raveling like fire in the embedded black stream, changing his mind and driving up the slope of sunny-looking Bermuda grass against the bight of the churning gray sky, to the old homesite, house rotting back into the earth among wild plum whips, a starveling pear and a mammoth pecan tree, old farm implements, stacks of tin and lumber and bricks, talking to her, "Hey, you awright?" Rain stinging his back like bees, he gets out at the slumped wire fence, between the pear and pecan trees, and loads her onto his right shoulder like a sack of cow feed. "Hey, hey, you awright?" Stepping over the fence and walking straight up to the caved-in brick well, knitted over with withy Bermuda grass and briers, and dumping her body, feet first, into the hole. Hearing crying, somebody crying, with the soft *whump* of her body landing, crumpling, on the bricks below, armloads of thatch stuffed into the hole—don't want to hurt her—thatch till the navy no longer shows, then the *clunk clunk clunk* of more bricks lowered inside, and a shrieking sheet of tin snarked from a nearby stack to cover the well, hearing himself saying, "Hey, hey, you awright?"

2

In the quarters, in his trailer, in his bed, he prays for more rain, "Lord, let it rain," shaking and moaning low. He had taken a break from moaning when he first got home. Just long enough to face up to his mama in the doorway of her midnight-blue trailer, across the close yard from his own trailer. "You awright?" she'd said, and he'd said, "Yep, just resting," words he'd been hoping to hear all afternoon.

"Sound like that bad dope done burnt up your brain," she said to him, and then to the mutinous children inside, "Y'all hush up now!"

Roper's red cur with the plume tail sidled around his legs, sniffing, while a stray, black and rust-pied with mange, sniffed the red cur's rump, then settled back on his haunches and scratched at his bony neck, knuckles drubbing out a rhythm on the sumpy dirt. Wet-dog and sour-mud stench. Houseflies swarmed around the dogs, around his mama's old white station wagon, around a white table cobbled with fish scales and Roper's junk collection on exhibit before Louise's trailer, the whole yard a junk heap contained by a circular hedge of bamboos and bushes.

"I mean knock off to rest," Roper said, "raining."

"You be in more trouble and that probate man come and get you."

She looked campy yet queenly in her dipped-hem lavender skirt and peasant shirt with a lavender scarf wound round her gray hair. A little knot of silk on the crest of the turban like a curl. One of many wild outfits she has taken as baby-sitting pay when the younger women in the quarters didn't, or said they didn't, have the money at the end of the week. Faddish clothes at odds with the scruff of old age, that tall warped frame and wrung face, hazel eyes reverting to the nickel-plated eyes of infancy.

"If the man come," said Roper and started walking with his plaid shirt slung over his shoulder, "I ain't here."

"What bout Little Taylor?"

"I ain't here." Halfway across the yard, Roper stopped walking. "Tell Mr. Math I been here since dinnertime, but I ain't here now."

"Them bad boys you brung in the world ain't come home on the schoolbus thi'sevening. Wherebouts you reckon they be?"

"Up to no good," mumbled Roper. Then louder, "Bout got off over there at Ahab's, playing ball."

A circle of racket—babies bawling, children shouting, people laughing, TVs blabbing, gunfire—sounded from the start of the sandy dirt road, at the highway, all the way around the loop to the end of the road and the hot hissing wheels of semis, northbound and southbound, on Highway 129 again. No quiet in spite of the surround of pines and hardwoods, where varicolored junked cars squat on their rims like blocks of flowering weeds.

She shook her long-jointed finger at Roper. "Go tell them boys I say keep away from that juke. Don't, they get to hanging with the wrong kind."

"I'm wet, Mama." Roper made a big show of raising his slack-skinned face to the rain.

"Ain't gone get no wetter," she said and talked on through the rain as if the sun was shining. "You don't show them boys who the boss, they end up like you and Walleyed Willie and Boss and them."

"I look like them boys' mama?" he said. "She the one walk off and leave em. Sides, I don't hang out with nobody no more."

"I be them boys' mama now, only mama they ever know. But you they daddy. Now go tell em I say . . ." A tiny boy with square hair ducks around her skirt and she grabs his stick arm to keep him from tumbling out the door.

"You go tell em what you say," said Roper.

"I bout done with telling," she said and stepped back with the child into her trailer with the paint-blackened windows. "Bout done with telling lies for you too."

He stalked off through the slashing rain toward his rusting brown trailer, set lengthwise in the yard, front pointed toward the hedge gap as if he is ready to haul it out anytime. But he never would go, because he never has gone—wouldn't know where or how—though he had almost been drafted during the Vietnam War—bad back saved him—and going to jail in Valdosta, twenty miles away, had been too far from home, too unsettling, had made the commotion of the quarters seem like static by comparison. Two rotting brown stuffed reclining chairs are propped against the north end of his trailer, under semiprotection, semiconcealment of the umbrella chinaberry overhead. This side of the ragged hedge between his trailer and Sweet's yard, where he parks

Taylor's pickup—can't park in his own yard for junk, can't park in his own yard for creating suspicion when the man comes—where he goes when he needs to, where he used to go when he wanted to. Woman ain't nothing but trouble.

He is short and stringy and gaunt, too old to need women, too old to want to go.

Passing through the low, warped door of his trailer, he could still hear his mama mumbling, grumbling, behind the windows painted black to keep from viewing the quarters' filth and sin. In the late sixties, when she had painted the windows of her new used trailer black, it had been to make a statement to her neighbors that she neither liked them nor wanted to be liked by them and preferred to remember the quarters the way they were before the Freedom Riders came in the mid-sixties and everything changed from neat to nasty, as she said. But Roper was damned if he could figure whether she loved or hated those students from Upnorth who came urging everybody to register to vote, which she and she alone ended up doing, though everybody else swore they would do, and he himself had tried to do, but buckled under after the Freedom Riders had left Swanoochee County and the quarters were burned and the men whipped. Yes, only Louise had ended up registering to vote. Only Louise had not buckled under. Only Louise kept singing "We shall o-ver-co-ome, we shall o-ver-co-ome . . ." and telling those lies that didn't jibe with the way Roper remembered it because he was fucked up and didn't even know he was fucked up—brain concussion—and had to be told, lies which she was probably telling the children right now, in full story form, though she never talks about any of it to

adults. Appears now to have buckled under too, but Roper
knows her—crazy woman!—and pities the children whom
he despises simply because they make him nervous.

The minute he closed his door, he started moaning
and shaking again while the rain rapped on the roof and
sheeted down the double windows facing Louise's trailer.
He knew she couldn't hear him and he could moan as
loud as he wanted, needed. But he kept it low, sounded
like his stomach growling. Even lying across the bed, he
kept up the same strangled moaning while the rain
whipped at the walls and roof like the dread whipping at
his mind.

❖ ❖ ❖

Roper doesn't know when he stopped moaning, he
doesn't know when the rain let up, but when he wakes it
is dark and he can hear over the grinding rattle of his
refrigerator motor, somebody knocking on his door. The
racket of the quarters—music from the juke and babies
crying—and somebody knocking on his door.

"Hey!" he says, jacking his head up from the pillow.

Bap bap bap.

"Hey," he says again, heartbeat on hold.

He eases up from the bed with his hands pressed down
on the mattress to keep the springs from squeaking.
Creeping across the sloped floor to the window over the
table and peeping through the dumpster-bargain bamboo blinds.

Outside, somebody shuffles, hugs the wall. Dark next
door, always dark, blackened windows. Dark yard except
for starts of starlight through the rocking branches of the
chinaberry tree.

Bap bap bap.

He tiptoes to the door, leaning against it and listening. Sniggering, *bap bap bap* on the outer wall's floppy siding.

He has to open the door now that he has spoken. Whoever it is—Taylor or the man (probation officer) or the sheriff—they know he is inside. They are onto him. But he doesn't believe they could have found the body so soon. He puts on his innocent face, which is innocent-looking anyway with his drooped mouth and eyes without putting on. He looks like a basset pup.

He cracks the door, just a slit. Opens it wider. Peeps out. Nothing. Nobody. Just cold pine air scouring the trailer's musty damp.

Then suddenly two heads with blood dripping from tongues and eyes. "Trick or treat!" Ha ha ha!

Roper steps back, holding his on-hold heart. Sprawling with relief in a brown plaid chair by the door. "Y'all get on out from here," he says to the boys. "Git!"

"The man come get Mr. Math's ugly old Zuzu," says Bloop, fourteen years old with legs like tomwalkers. "Say he seen you out driving with no fucking license." Ha ha ha!

"I say git!" Roper jumps up, grabs the truck keys from the table and pockets them. "I ain't say y'all can come in here."

"What you got?" says Bloop, fake blood dripping from his smooth black chin to his Grateful Dead T-shirt. "We thirsty."

"RC in the icebox," says Roper.

Both boys laugh.

White caps, white shirts, white shoes, white teeth. Bloop bebops across the rust-ringed beige tiles of the living room to the adjoining kitchen, to the rusty, squat refrigerator on the south wall. The whole trailer is done in rust tones—dumpster quality—and even the refrigerator has rust-smelling breath.

Bloop yanks on the latch of the refrigerator.

"Look out you don't snatch that icebox off its block," says Roper.

Too late. The refrigerator slides forward, side-tilted with door gaping, and growls like a wildcat.

"What you wanta move out of Granmama place for?" says Bloop, surveying the sorry trailer.

"One thing, to get away from y'all," says Roper. "Shut that door. Lean on it and kick that block back under there."

Bloop lifts up on the left side of the refrigerator and toes the thin square of wood under the left corner. "Man, when I grow up I'm gone be rich. Ain't living in no dump like this."

"Shut the door," says Roper. "Ain't nothing but RC to drink in there."

"Yeah, but you got dope, I bet," says Beanie, kicking in the carpet of old clothes and papers along the west wall. Twelve years old, he looks younger, looks shorter in over-sized khaki shorts and white T-shirt, and small in clunky white running shoes. Cream-brown skin the shade of Roper's, he is almost as tall as Roper.

"I tell yo granmama you messing with dope and she have yo heads."

"She ain't fucking studying us."

"Hand over the keys so we can go out trick or treating," Beanie says.

"You touch that truck and you in a mess of trouble," Roper says.

"You mean *you* in a mess of trouble." Ha ha ha! Bloop is back, standing before Roper and squeezing more fake blood from a small plastic tube, dabbing it under his eyes, his fat lips.

Beanie slides down the west wall to the clothes heap, and sits holding his knees. "For a fact, Mr. Math been by."

Roper checks Beanie's eyes for signs of lying, though he still can't tell. Not anymore. "What he say?"

"Say he just want to ask you something."

"He ask if I work thi'sevening?"

"Ain't say nothing else," says Beanie, resetting his white cap backward, "just take off in that white Chevy stepside."

Bloop is standing in the open door now. Crowding Roper's space. "We clearing out," he says and shoots to the dirt. The trailer wobbles.

"Y'all go picking at people," says Roper, "and I ain't getting you out of trouble no more."

"Like the last time, huh?" Beanie scoots forward, stands, springs out the door.

"Just don't be messing with Mr. Math truck."

"That fucking old Zuzu! Huh!" says Beanie, weaving among the puzzle pieces of mud puddles glimmering with stars.

3

Monday morning, with frost on the road shoulders and the sun sneaking somewhere beyond the pinesline, Roper has to cruise back and forth along 129, between the quarters and Taylor's place, and risk the man catching him driving, to keep from showing up for work too early (he has always been late) and looking guilty of killing the woman he didn't kill. Daylight Savings Time had changed to Eastern Standard Time on Sunday and messed him up. He wouldn't have known about the time changing if his mama hadn't dropped by on her way to church to tell him that Math Taylor had been by looking for him. Again. Said Little Taylor sure takes after his daddy, who she never will forget going to that evening forty some-odd years ago when he decided to get out of the cotton business, and asking him to let the farmhands and their families stay on in the quarters. Nowhere else to go, she'd said, and he'd said, "Louise, don't you reckon your people would be better off to move on since ain't nothing for them to do here now?" ("Your people" was how Wainer Taylor always referred to the labor, because Louise was the time and weight keeper for Taylor's cotton farm in the fifties; Louise was a good hand to write.) Then he went into the turpentine business and changed the farmhands into turpentine hands and everybody lived happily ever after till ... She stopped in the middle of her history-lesson-turned-fantasy and said to Roper, "Why you be moaning and taking on so?"

Last time turning around at the dumpster, south of the railroad overpass, from which point Roper could see the sun rising like a blistered peach at the apex of rails, and he heads north. Driving slow and scooching low, he keeps his right foot even on the gas pedal (up and down and he'll look guilty). When the Isuzu crests the hill, where Taylor's white house sits back off the highway, Roper can see through the screen of mossy oaks that the house is dark and still, that Math Taylor's white Chevy pickup and his wife's green Volvo are parked on the north side of the house.

Roper gears the Isuzu to second and coasts through the island of oaks, along the south side of the house, and straight up the pond road. Frost like banked snow on the section of unmowed weeds, and frost like level snow on the mowed section of weeds. Except for a few frost bumps on weeds the mower had missed, which Roper had never noticed before. Lots of fresh tracks, tire and shoe prints, on the road to the pond: Easy driving and white-knuckling the steering wheel, he has to tear his eyes from the old homesite with its falling-down house and barn. He can't see the well site for the trees, but he thinks he can see the sheet of tin with frost glittering in the sun now peeking over the east woods.

At the tractor, he unlatches the icy hood, lifts it, checks the oil, climbs up, engages the choke, then turns the switch key—eyes shifting from the tin to the still-dark house. When the tractor starts, white smoke puffs from the exhaust pipe on the hood, and the soothing familiar *clata-clat-clat* sets the morning in motion as he picks up mowing where he'd left off on Friday, picks up moaning where he'd left off this morning. Mowing on toward the house, where now a single light glows yellow in one of the rear windows.

Two more turns from the house to the pond, almost to the road where the woman had been lying, and on his way back toward the house he can see that the white pickup is gone from its parking place. At the pond turn, he steers the tractor south, toward the road that runs around the property—he will go to the old homesite and see if the sheet of tin has been moved—but suddenly spies the white pickup across the rainbow glitter of frost, gliding in the sun slant up the road toward the pond.

He yanks the tractor round, leveling it with the row of unmowed weeds, and heads toward the Taylor house. Breathing hard with his face prickling like frostbite.

When the pickup stops on the road, directly in line with Roper, he stops the tractor, gets off and starts lope-walking toward the truck, meeting Math Taylor halfway. A giant blond man wearing a white cap and blue jeans and a tan corduroy jacket with a fleecy collar. Weeds crunching under both their feet, with the *clata-clat-clat* of the idling tractor passing over the field in echo.

"Roper," says Taylor, pocketing his hands and planting one work boot solid on the furrow ahead.

"How you, Mr. Math?"

"Ain't no good this morning, Roper."

"Sho turnt off cold, ain't it?"

"Killing frost."

"Sho is now."

"What time you knock off last Friday, Roper?"

"Dinnertime," says Roper. "Set in to raining so I stay at the house."

"Yeah." Math Taylor twists, looking toward the pond. "Didn't happen to see the wife before you left, did you?"

"Talk to her up to the house," says Roper, "told her I was gone get some of that gas out of a can there." Roper points toward the tin shed to the right of the pecan orchard.

"That'd been just before dinnertime?"

"Yessir," says Roper. "Didn't see no point in coming back and it raining."

Math Taylor spells him with wide aqua eyes, red etched. "That's all right bout you not coming back; it's just we got this problem—Lora went missing sometime last Friday."

"Missing?"

"Nobody ain't laid eyes on her since I left Friday morning. I mean but you."

"She awright when I see her."

"Well, she ain't now." Math Taylor coughs into his right fist, pockets his hand again. "Looks like she just up and walked off. Clothes is still here. Car's still here. Law's been looking all over, putting a all-points bulletin out on her today." He spits to the side. "Beginning to figger somebody picked her up on the highway when she went out walking. Bad about walking that highway, stead of the field road like I told her. Snakes crawling this time of year, and she was . . . is . . . scared to death of snakes." He stops talking, swallows, reddish beard like thorns in the bright sun. That thick, fair neck.

Roper tries to think of something to say, tries to keep his eyes from straying to the sun-shimmering tin capping the well.

"I talked to her on the telephone Friday morning, round eleven," says Taylor. "Then our girl lives in Valdosta talked to her later, bout dinnertime. Said her mama wadn't feeling good, had some chest pains and whatall, was going out walking, see if that'd help."

Again he stops talking, but doesn't seem to be waiting for Roper to speak, doesn't seem to be trying to trick him. Just thinking. "Don't make no sense," says Taylor.

Roper spot-checks the tin, the brightening sky, the place where the woman with the chest pains lay last Friday. Starts to tell all he knows but instead says, "You want me to keep on mowing?" Trick of the mouth.

"Yeah," says Math Taylor, turning, "bout as well. Just keep on mowing till you get to that patch of pines off the creek yonder." He motions toward the creek beyond the old homesite. Then starts walking back toward his truck with his broad shoulders slumped, his long stride short-ened by stepping furrow to furrow.

Roper strolls back toward the tractor.

"Hey, Roper," Taylor calls, stopping and looking around, "if that bad tractor tire gets low of air, fill it up with water and see if we can't get a little more use out of it. And if you see anything suspicious, how bout letting me know?"

"Sho will." Roper keeps the same brisk, breezy gait till he gets to the tractor, then swings up and drives forward, eyes fixed on the road where the white Chevy will pass on its way out of the field. When it doesn't come before Roper reaches the turnaround in the pecan orchard, he expects to see it at the old homesite. But is more shocked to see it on the road adjacent to the tractor. So close he can make out Taylor's troubled face.

❖ ❖ ❖

By midmorning the white pickup is gone from its parking spot at the house, the frost has burned from the field, and the sheet of tin on the well is shining like water.

Bony shoulders hiked, Roper mows the last row of weeds along the north side of the road, then crosses to the south side and begins mowing west to east with the tin shed south of the house as a gauge. Good to be giving up the house with the green car as a gauge, good to be by himself again with the *clata-clat-clat* of the tractor, which sounds quieter with the white Chevy gone. But the old homesite, still a few hundred yards away, soon becomes Roper's main gauge and reminder. He watches the sky where blue jays streak, and the rows of pines running from the pond to the south end of the field. The sun, when he turns, is like a cold, white explosion in the clear, blue sky. A couple of jet trails, like chalk rubbed sideways. And then buzzards wheeling high over the old homesite.

Moaning loud, he hops from the tractor, leaving it idling, feet keeping beat with the *clata-clat-clat* as he races across the field, loping high over cold-cured grass and briers till he reaches the sunken roof section at the rear of the old house. Easing first along the slumped wire fence, then stepping over, around an old-timey chopper and a notched sawmill blade, sniffing and smelling nothing but rooty dirt and cold, and hearing only grasshoppers clicking in the dry grass and the squeaky-hinge sound of smoky doves. At the well, he lifts the tin without looking inside and drags it back to the pile next to the chopper, moving fast and thinking fast, and lugs stacks of bricks to the well and dumps them inside, over and over and not looking but listening till the plops turn to solid thunks, and then he looks, and then he sees specks of navy or maybe dark spangles before his eyes, and goes back for more bricks, dumping them in till they reach almost ground level.

Cream-brown face bright with sweat, he can see himself in the reflection of tin as he snarks sheets over the bare dirt bed where the bricks have left their rectangular imprints. Kicking thatch and dead leaves over his tracks, he starts back, watching the pond road for the white truck and the sky for the silent buzzards still lassoing the air and circling just to be circling.

Instead of going home for lunch, he sits in the cab of the pickup with his head back and dozes. And in a skimming dream replays all he has been through since last Friday, all that has happened, and decides that if he hadn't buried the body under bricks he might still have an out—he could have told Math Taylor the truth. But knows he still can tell or that he never would have told in the first place.

"I ain't kill her," he says, sitting up and spying the glint of sun off another automobile in the sideyard of the Taylor house, and another one in the shade, which might have a blue light bar on top if Roper can trust his tricky eyesight. From where he sits, pointed east, he has a clear view of the tall white house with its hovering green oaks and gray moss, the blanched stubble of the mowed north field, the pinewoods behind in the rearview mirror, and in the south, the old homesite with the well with the body, and his trail leading to it. His vision fans out over the entire two hundred acres, and he'd like to stay forever, keeping watch over his own undoing.

"Gotta keep mowing," he says and eases open the truck door, eases it shut, and lopes toward the tractor.

With every round he is erasing his trail of broken weeds to the old homesite—not that his trail is all that visible except to him. Each time up and down the field, he tries to pick out his trail and can—like a deer path. He has to keep mowing. He has to keep moving.

Almost sundown and the strange cars still sit on the north side of the house, and Roper seems no closer to the old homesite, though he has to be. He will mow on till dark, but if he does, Math Taylor might get suspicious—Roper always knocks off right at five. But five now, Eastern Standard, suntime, is like six Daylight Savings Time.

Eastbound on the tractor through the shallow fog called rabbits' smoke, level with the old homesite, and the engine begins sputtering, the wheels chug over and stop. He looks down at the gas gauge and the red needle is slanted all the way over to the E mark behind the cloudy plastic disk. Which means that tomorrow Roper will have to get Taylor to gas up. Which means this evening Roper will have to leave the tractor next to the old homesite like a marker saying HERE.

On his way out, at the oak island in the front yard, Roper has to suck in to keep from moaning: a van marked WALB TV is parked in front of the house, with a camera crew and cameras spilling from the rear double doors; a brown sheriff's car with a still blue light bar on top is parked next to it; and two strange cars with men, women, and children standing round are parked on the north yard, next to the green Volvo and the white Chevy stepside. They stare at him, guilty in the blue Isuzu Pup.

4

In retrospect, for the most part, Lora Taylor had seemed decently deceased, one more person who had died of some natural cause, or vanished, and everybody acquainted with the deceased could get on with their lives. For Roper, that is, until the TV news this morning. He hasn't known how deeply he has sensed that till he sees her too-rose face—an old picture—on his mama's off-hue TV screen and realizes that the search will go on. Last evening, they had dragged the pond, found nothing. The only thing Roper has going for him, so far, is the fact that the search appears to be focused away from the Taylor place, since the pond dragging, rather than on the Taylor place. Official speculation is Mrs. Taylor had gone out walking along Highway 129 and somebody had abducted her. According to her husband, Math Taylor, his wife had been complaining of chest pains, which she admitted to her daughter in a phone conversation shortly before her disappearance. Though Taylor is not considered a suspect at this time, he is being interrogated by local officials. Taylor claims to have been working on a construction site in Valdosta last Friday, but has failed to provide an alibi. Employees for Taylor say he left the job site around noon and never returned. According to Taylor, after knocking off for lunch, he went by Wal-Mart, and when the rain started he decided to take off for the rest of the day. Roper Rackard, a black man hired to mow the fields on Taylor's Swanoochee County farm, was the last person to see Lora Taylor, sometime around noon on Friday. Rackard will be questioned later today.

Hearing his name officially announced by the TV man with thatchy gray hair makes Roper sit up stiff in the chair by the door of his mama's trailer. Makes her turn and eye him as she straggles in from the kitchen, one lap baby in her arms and a toddler clinging to her fuchsia knit pants leg, stepping around the sprawl of whining children on quilt pallets before the TV. Roper doesn't even blink. Not even when she stops to the left of the TV set, mumbling, and parts the curtains on the windows painted black. Might be night for all the light is allowed inside. Overhead lights on in the middle of the morning.

Even before hearing his name on TV, Roper had made up his mind not to go to work today. He will go to see the man today. Why he had come over to his mama's trailer in the first place, to get her to drive him to Valdosta. He won't come back. He hopes he won't come back. He has never been farther west than Valdosta, Georgia, never farther south than Jasper, Florida, and north and east about the same timid distance. He has twenty dollars in his pockets, enough for a bus ticket to Somewhere, and his seventy-five-dollar fine installments are paid up till the end of November, but if he leaves the law will be after him for breaking probation. If he leaves now the law will be after him for killing the woman he didn't kill. What he might do, though he cannot imagine it, is turn himself in to the man. Just walk right up to his probation officer and tell him the truth, but the man behind the desk in Roper's mind picture doesn't look as if he would believe Roper if he told either truth or lie.

❖ ❖ ❖

At the probation office, a white brick building cold-shaded with live oaks, Roper leaves his mama and the scrapping, tumbling children in her old white station wagon and passes through the front door, taking a right at the empty desk where a white woman usually sits, and ducks down the hall with an EXIT sign at the end, and left into the restroom. Usually, Roper would stop and study the sign to be sure he didn't go into the one marked WOMEN, but not this time. This time he walks straight into one of the two cubicles and sits fully clothed on the toilet and stares at the white door with a penknife scratch reading SHIT and kneads his bony knees. Same kneading motion his mama's long-jointed hands had been making on the station wagon's steering wheel since they left the quarters, while monitoring the big kids/little kids battle in the backseat and grumbling about "them boys" heading out to school in shorts that morning and catching cold. He would like to have told her that colds couldn't catch Bloop and Beanie, fast and bad as they are, and the possibility that they are in school today is no possibility at all. He would like to have told her next time that brat she calls Little Angel conks him on the head with her bottle he is going to send her to heaven. Louise never mentioned the TV news about the missing woman, about her son's upcoming questioning; but then, Roper concludes, anybody who would paint their windows black to keep from seeing bad would probably stopper their ears to keep from hearing bad. Besides, she is old, old and weary.

from seeing and hearing. Might be going deaf, for all he knows. And her trailer is always brimming with the racket of brats, trying to outblast the blasting TV. But Roper would bet a million dollars she knows. Is she waiting for him to bring it up, to confess?

Somebody swings through the restroom door and settles into the next cubicle, a woman's black high heels and slim, stockinged ankles. Roper sucks in, waiting.

After the woman has left, Roper gets up, flushes the toilet, and starts out, taking a left toward the side exit, going out into the bright sunshine, intending to trek on around the building to the Trailways bus station, next street over, but instead heads for the front and the white station wagon and his mama, and feels relieved though damned.

"The man ain't in," he says and opens the car door and gets in, nudging over a tiny boy with a living line of yellow snot from his nose to his lips. "Woman say come back tomorrow," Roper adds and shuts the door. Sometimes he does that, and if his mama knows she never mentions it, just starts the car, backing feebly onto the street she will drive tomorrow and tomorrow till Roper gets over his case of nerves or laziness, or has to report in for real, for his monthly visit with the man.

❖ ❖ ❖

Like the quarters' dogs, Roper's boys flock to his mama's car as she pulls into the yard. Dribbling basketballs on the hard-packed dirt, they grin. "Ain't no school today, no ma'am," Bloop says to his grandmother, *ploong ploong plap*—basketball bouncing off the side of Roper's rust trailer.

"Git on out from here," says Roper, slumping from the car to the circle shade of the chinaberry, where the red cur is sleeping on its side. Except for one ear twitching as the front door slams at Sweet's house, beyond the hedge, the dog looks dead.

"Shurf been here, man," says Beanie, "him and Mr. Math looking for you."

Roper had been about to go through his door, but stops without turning. Says nothing.

"Wanting to talk to you bout that missing white woman."

"You boys get on bout your meanness," says Louise in her braying voice, then mumbling to the children bailing out of the car, or to the air—"Shurf in the quarters ain't never mean nothing but trouble"—and starts herding the children toward her trailer.

"You tell em I had to go see the man?" Roper asks Bloop.

"We ain't say nothing," says Bloop, *ploong ploong plap*— the basketball bounces from the wall on Roper's right.

"Give us the key to that Zuzu, man," says Bloop, and bounces the ball off the hood of the Isuzu parked over the spindly hedge of the next yard—next yard in case the man should come. "We wanting to go to the fair."

"Ain't nobody touching that truck," says Roper.

"You say you'll take us."

"I say if you go to school like somebody, I take you."

"Man, you in some kind of trouble!" says Beanie with his oversized shorts hanging miraculously low on his butt.

"I know it," says Roper and steps through the door, closing it.

❖ ❖ ❖

He waits on the edge of the bed, alternately watching through the peephole window on the west wall the butchered sun bleed out behind the roof of Sweet's house and resting his head in his hands. When Math Taylor and the sheriff come, he will tell them the truth.

He has even changed his socks—can't stand nasty socks—and placed his pocketknife on the table with Taylor's truck key. He will tell the truth, though the truth sounds like a lie even to him. What he dreads most— other than the other jailbirds—is the shocked look on Taylor's face when he learns that all along Roper was guilty and begins replaying in his mind every word Roper said on Monday when Taylor questioned him about his missing wife.

"One aggravating white woman," Roper says aloud.

While he waits, he listens to the music from the juke on the east curve of the quarters swell around the voices of Sweet and Lucy, in the yard next door. Jabbering, jabbering about the Florida lottery—once a week Lucy drives to the Florida line and picks up lottery tickets for herself and Sweet—which somehow leads into talk of the missing woman. "Mr. Math bout done got him a young woman," says Sweet. "Get that marble outta that baby mouth! Bout done knock his old lady in the head and dump her in the river."

"Look to me like don't matter where he done it or didn't," says Lucy, "plenty of people round Swanoochee County like to lay it to him."

Sweet: "Git on out from here!" (Dogs or children?)

"TV say she be bad bout walking the hardroad," Lucy

says. "Ain't no tellings," her voice moving now. "Lota meanness nowdays; see it everday up yonder at the Valdosta hospital. Gotta go pick up the younguns from Miss Louise."

Time out from straining to hear: a freight train whistles in the west, rumble and toot coming like a tornado; close, it quakes the floor, then rumbles out east. Gone. Roper listens for the going-on sounds in the quarters to hear whether the sheriff has come with the train. Maybe gone too.

The boys shout, yodel-laugh, basketballs whumping on the hard dirt under the chinaberry tree. Taking turns shooting balls at the netless hoop Roper had brought home from the dumpster across the overpass and nailed to the tree. Hearing them on into the dusk, then the dark, with dogs barking and people laughing and TVs playing out the same situations house to house along the loop. Women stopping by to pick up their children from Louise's trailer. Roper is still listening out, trying to sort the regular traffic sounds from the irregular sounds of a strange car—he always listens for strange automobiles, and usually will be standing at the door, ready. Say, the man might be coming by to see him. Well, not always standing ready, not till after he got caught for selling dope. Walleyed Willie and Boss, the big boys, never even got busted; Roper just happened to be in the juke when Ahab got raided for selling beer on Sunday. Only the second time Roper had ever sold crack cocaine—never even used it himself. Try telling that to the man.

Two hours into dark, getting hungry, smelling bacon, maybe corned beef hash, cooking at his mama's trailer, Roper is ready to give up his waiting for the night, but hears that strange car he's been waiting to hear slowing on 129 and turning onto the dirt road. He stands up, patting his empty pockets, places his twenty-dollar bill on the table and starts out, but sits again on the edge of the bed. While listening to Bloop and Beanie talking to Math Taylor and the sheriff, Roper indulges in one last look around the trailer furnished with dumpster furniture and knickknacks. Home.

"Hey, Roper," yells Bloop, "shurf here to see you." Then the *blam blam blam* of Bloop's fist on the metal wall, making Roper jump. He coughs, stands, goes to the door, and swings out around Bloop hugging his basketball. Seeing the brown car with the cold light bar on top parked in the opening of circular bushes and the two men standing before the front bumper. Math Taylor with one work boot propped, and the sheriff, clean and stout, with crossed arms and legs, leaning against the hood. Both backlit by the fake-moon security lights in Lucy's yard across the road. Sagging clotheslines of dingy wash, like headless, limbless ghosts of the people Roper sees every day.

"Roper," says Taylor, "shurf here wants to ask you a few questions about Miss Lora."

"Done tole all I know," says Roper, bounce-walking toward them.

"I know that," says Taylor, zipping his tan corduroy coat with the fleecy collar. "Law just has to take it down in writing. For the record."

Roper stops before the sheriff and Math Taylor, wringing his crossed arms and twisting, while behind him the boys dribble basketballs, and his mama stands solid in the lit doorway of her trailer.

"How you, Mama Lou?" says Taylor.

"Ain't much," she says. "How you doing, Little Taylor?"

"Well, I been better."

"I ain't forget you."

"I know that, Mama Lou. I prechate that. And prechate that good pound cake you sent by Roper last week." Taylor switches his wide aqua eyes from Louise to Roper, as if to put an end to the aimless chitchat. Get on with business.

"Had to go up there and see the man today," says Roper. "How come I ain't work today."

"Just be there tomorrow," says Taylor, dropping it. His red face has a purplish cast produced by a tattoo-work of veins branching from his temples to his fleshy cheeks. Gray-blond hair curling over the rim of his white Jack Daniels cap.

The sheriff leans sideways on the car front so that his brass badge shows on his stuffed khaki shirt. Khaki pants twisting on his stout legs as he places one foot on the bumper, studying Roper. "Taylor says you seen his wife bout dinnertime last Friday, that so?"

"Not but a minute, I didn't. Not but a minute. It be making up to rain and I come on to the house." Roper crooks his right arm behind him and scratches his back with his thumb.

"Where was she when you seen her?"

"She be in the house, I mean out of the house. She come out of the house for me to say I was fixing to get some of Mr. Math's gas from that can under the shed. To get home on. I say . . ."

"She seem all right?"

"Sir? Yessir, seem awright to me, what little bit I see her.

She go on back in the house bout the time I get in the truck. It come *some kind a rain* bout dinnertime . . . how come I didn't go on back to work." Roper rubs beneath his nose with his forefinger, waiting for the sheriff to speak, waiting for the bogged gray eyes of the sheriff to shift, then lets the words flow to fill space. "You a good man, Mr. Math, sho nuf be good to me. I don't aim to short you on my work time."

"So," says the sheriff, planting both feet on the ground but still leaning sideways, "you didn't go back out to Taylor's place once you got done eating dinner?"

"Nawsuh, sho didn't. Mama there be my witness I ain't leave the house no more that day." Roper nods toward his mama in the doorway without looking. Then laughs and wags his head. "The man catch me driving, I be in trouble big time." He looks back at his mama, loud in a chartreuse jumpsuit but mum as Sunday, and when he looks at the sheriff and Taylor again, he spies his old dope-dealing buddies, Walleyed Willie and Boss, standing on the white sand road defined by security lights along the loop. Same way they do when Math Taylor comes to pay Roper on Fridays. In the shadows of other yards and along the trash-bound road, Roper can spot men, women, and children, moving, standing, listening. Kick-shy dogs slinking.

"Ain't nobody after you over this, Roper," says Math Taylor. "Ain't nobody believes you done nothing."

Roper glances aside at his trailer, at the Isuzu roof shining over the hedge in Sweet's porch light, at the boys' greased movements across the dirt yard. Dribbling round the long white table cluttered with pots and cans and a statuette of a headless naked woman with a vase sprouting from her left shoulder. Sweet and about half the quarters have gathered on her front porch. Not a sound, except for the *blap blap blap* of the basketballs and Roper's heart.

The sheriff, still eyeballing Roper, walks gamely around to the driver's side of the car. Opens the door and props his left arm on top. "I tell you what, Rackard, a man looks as guilty as you do pro'bly ain't."

Taylor walks around the car. Talking over the light bar to the sheriff, "You scared him's all," he says and gets in. "See you in the morning, Roper."

The sheriff works his body in under the steering wheel, starts the car and backs out, talking to Roper through the open window. "If you come up with something might help this *good man* out, Rackard, how bout letting us know? He's bout worried hisself to death over this thing."

Roper bounce-walks, smiling and nodding, toward his trailer, opens the door and goes inside and flops in his chair. In a few minutes, after the smooth roar of the sheriff's car has faded and the basketball heartbeats stop, a soft knock sounds on Roper's door, which he recognizes as his mama's warning that she's coming in ready or not. The door opens and they lock eyes.

She looks cold, frail and foolish in the chartreuse jumpsuit, like a man dressed up in women's clothes. "You kill Miss Lora?" she says, standing stiff in the doorway with the streaked light at her back.

"No um."

"You know what went with her?"

"No um."

"I belief the first answer, but not the last." She starts to walk away. She stops. "If you didn't know something, you wouldn't had to story like that."

"Truth ain't gone change nothing for Mr. Math, Mama. Just for me."

"Little Taylor been good to us—Big Taylor too. Been sho nuf good to you."

"I know it."

"How come you didn't take off when you could this morning?"

"This be the onliest place I know, Mama, right here. Ain't done nothing wrong."

She turns, her roughened voice walking. "Ain't done nothing right neither."

❖ ❖ ❖

The crown of Roper's head, jammed into the paneled wall, aches when he wakes to the sound of his red cur growling beneath the floor under his bed. Roper is sleeping with his bare rump up in the cool dank air, on his knees, rocking and groaning. He rolls over and rubs his face, sees the room is still dark, that it's still night, except for a rectangle of fake moonlight through the narrow north window above his bed. Familiar smells of rotting walls, like week-old flower water in a vase, and cigarette smoke. No sound inside except for his refrigerator's normal about-to-quit roar, and outside, a tuneless trickle.

Kneeling on the mattress, he peers through the window, nose pressed to the dusty screen, and sees the silhouettes of two men—one short and stocky and the other tall—standing next to the Isuzu on Sweet's side of the hedge. He crawls across the bed, steps into his pants, and tips barefoot from the bedroom to the living room.

At the door, he lifts up on the knob as he turns it and stills the rattley chain that keeps the door from swinging all the way out.

The cur slides on her belly from beneath the trailer, stretches and shakes the dust from her short red fur, then rubs up against Roper's legs. He places one hand on her heart-shaped head and bends low and eases along the hedge. Eyes on the Isuzu, eyes on the men—four, counting shadows.

Close enough to reach across the bushy hedge and touch the left headlamp of the Isuzu, he can see a five-gallon can on the dirt next to the driver's door and a length of garden hose trailing from the gas tank's mouth to the spout of the can. Slow-gurgling gas.

Not the first time somebody has siphoned gas from the Isuzu, and Roper would like to just creep back inside and pretend he doesn't know and tell Taylor when he comes by to check on Roper tomorrow that the reason he didn't show up for work was because somebody had stolen all the gas again. No sweat. But under the circumstances, Roper decides it's best to keep things running smoothly, on course—the course Roper can feel but can't foresee taking shape. Going to work tomorrow morning, for starters, which he hadn't planned on doing but just knows it feels right or at least less suspicious looking.

He stands tall, face to face with Walleyed Willie so close he can see the fried-egg whites of the other man's eyes.

Walleyed Willie elbows Boss, who has one hand propped on the Isuzu door and the other holding the gurgling hose.

In the gutted light from Lucy's yard across the road, Roper can see two star scars of bullet holes and about a half-dozen zipper scars from healed-over knifings on Boss's muscled belly. Black shirt unbuttoned and sleeves ripped from the shoulder seams. Roper can't see the 38 Special in the waistband of Boss's blue jeans, but knows if Boss is wearing his pants he is wearing his pistol.

"Mama know you out after dark?" Boss says low, still holding to the hose, still propping on the door. His malt-liquor breath weaves into the fumes of gas.

Walleyed Willie shifts feet, his broad shoulders drop, he laughs. His head is shaved and his glossy scalp looks like chocolate fudge before it sugars over.

"Ain't my gas you stealing, man," says Roper, hugging his bony ribcage. "It Mr. Math gas."

"No shitting," says Walleyed Willie, turning and unzipping and peeing on the hedge. Spattering Roper's cold feet.

"He done onto y'all," says Roper—lie. "Know y'all be into his gas. Know y'all take all but the tires off his truck."

"Uh huh," says Boss and yanks the hose from the gas tank and rolls it up and hands it to Walleyed Willie. Gas leaks from the hose to the grass and mingles with the piss. "Ain't make no call on us yet, is he?" He takes the gas cap from the dewy roof of the Isuzu and screws it back on tightly. Politely. Then screws the cap on the spout of the can.

"Look like Mr. Math got his hands full since you kill his old lady," says Boss.

The red cur wanders off to the flared shadow of the chinaberry tree, sits and scratches, scratches.

"I ain't kill nobody."

"What the law doing round here then?" says Walleyed Willie, zipping up and wheeling.

Roper toes the chilled dirt. "He know I ain't kill no white woman."

"What about that probate man? What you tell him bout us?" Boss lifts the can by the handle.

"Ain't tell him nothing," says Roper, adding, "yet."

Boss massages his right side, the pistol under his open black shirt. "We clean, man, ain't messing with no more dope. They got their eye on this place, cause of you." He walks off along the hedge toward the road with his left arm out to balance the heavy gas can in his right hand. "Tomorrow, fore you come home, how bout lifting a couple of chains from Taylor? Got a man need chains bad. Just leave em on back of the truck and we come get em tomorrow night."

"Y'all done steal the tow chain off the Isuzu, sell the man that."

"Done sell that one."

Roper sidles through the hedge and kicks at the left front tire and almost breaks his toe on the raped hub.

5

Wednesday and it is warming up to rain again, a bottom layer of sluffy gray clouds scudding beneath the iron girding of the sky, meaning rain will set in and stay awhile. Roper hopes so. But at the same time he hopes he can work a couple of days at least, get enough money to take the boys to the fair in Valdosta before it leaves next week. Help take his mind off his troubles and make good on his promise to them (same thing as promising Mama), though they have failed to make good on their promise to go to school every day.

He turns the pickup off 129, at Taylor's place, through the oak island and south of the house—only the green car, parked in its usual place—through the pecan grove and across the bumpy field toward the old homesite and the blue tractor. Eyes drawing toward the location of the sunken well that seems as obvious as a tower to Roper. He has bought five dollars' worth of tractor gas out of his own twenty-dollar bill, to keep from bothering Math Taylor in his time of grieving and have him visit so near the grave of the woman he is grieving.

Roper feels sharp, on top of things, one up on Boss and Walleyed Willie, because a while back Roper had started storing the spare tire of the Isuzu under his bed. Never mind that he had to borrow gas from Lucy's car after they left last night; never mind that this evening he will have to borrow that red chain hanging from a rafter of Taylor's tool shed. Roper doesn't know what his old buddies will do to him if he doesn't deliver (once he saw Walleyed Willie bite the head off a chicken while he was high on dope). Roper doesn't know what they have on him (sounded like they were trying to bluff him into believing that they knew he got rid of Lora Taylor's body). Maybe the dump-truck driver or the man in the rust-brown Pontiac told that Roper did go back to the Taylor place after lunch on Halloween day. But Roper does know he's never heard of somebody wanted to knock off Santa Claus.

To start the tractor, Roper has to spray ether into the intake manifold, a raw, cold smell on the ripe, warm air, and settles into his east-to-west pattern of mowing the soggy brown weeds and thrummy blond Bermuda grass. Watching the old house with the bowed shingle roof on the eastbound run and the planted pines on the west-bound run, and now and then the sky for buzzards. A flock of blackbirds over the old homesite rotates in flight toward the creek nook along the south woodsline. Sound of the tractor a familiar beating like the blood in Roper's ears, the sound of nothingness. Another couple of runs and Roper will be mowing close to the well, and he looks forward to and dreads it. What if he had told Taylor and the sheriff the truth, the way he had planned? What good would the truth have done Math Taylor, whose wife would still be dead? One thing for sure, though, the truth would have hurt Roper Rackard, who would right now be in the lockup with the other jailbirds instead of out here in the open with the blackbirds.

He begins to whistle in his usual tuneless way, though

usually he whistles only to let somebody know he is around. Way he used to do when he had to go to the Taylor house and could hear him and his wife fighting or whatever inside. Roper drives on past the grassed-over wellsite he has exposed by mowing the cover of weeds this side of the wire fence, between the stout-trunked pecan tree and the scraggly pear tree. Yeah, things are getting back to normal now. If the law hasn't found the woman's body by now they probably never will find it. Surely they have searched every foot of the fields and woods and are focusing on some other place, and before long Math Taylor will forget all about his wife (same old not-news on TV last evening). Taylor and his daughter might have some kind of memorial service for the woman Roper has saved them the expense and trouble of burying.

When the rain starts, a slow cool drizzle, Roper drives back to the Isuzu to get the hooded green vinyl jacket Math Taylor had given him, slips it on, and climbs back onto the wet tractor seat. Cold but not freezing and relieved to be working—makes him look genuinely interested in the job Math Taylor has created for him after he got into trouble for dealing drugs he was barely even dealing, and helps make him look less guilty of killing the woman he hasn't killed. Mowing all the way round the old homesite now, close along the broken rusty fence, which requires real concentration to keep the left tractor tire and mower edge free of the wire, he almost forgets about the woman entombed in the well.

On the next round, one tractor swath over from the fence, he feels, hears, glimpses something white sling from beneath the mower with the cut brown weeds and blond grass and looks back as he drives on, past the well and the pecan tree toward the span of board fence and an old cattle-loading chute on the south curve. Making the circle and heading back past the stack of tin and the fallen section of house, he has the same blood-draining feeling as when he'd first driven into the field last Friday and had seen Lora Taylor crumpled on the road near the pond—hoping he wasn't seeing what he thought he was seeing but knowing he was.

Getting closer to the narrow white something in the chopped weeds, one mower swath away, he can make out what looks like a white running shoe, gnawed by the mower blades. He shifts to neutral, gazes around at the open field where the rain slashes evenly across the neat mowed rows, climbs down from the tractor and idle-walks toward the white object. He picks it up, turning it in his hands: a right shoe, a woman's shoe, old-looking but not old-looking enough, the same shoe he'd seen on Lora Taylor's turned-inward foot last Friday.

"One aggravating white woman," he says.

Quickly he stuffs the shoe into the deep pocket of his coat, looking again across the hazy field. Moaning low and wondering what other evidence he might have deposited in the field when he carried her body from the truck to the well. Maybe another shoe, maybe a sock. No great mystery why the search party hadn't found it, not in this thicket of briers and fennels and grass. He has to keep mowing, searching, if it takes all day, rain or not.

He mows through dinnertime, in the increasing rain, eyes fixed on the weeds being chopped into thatch clumps by the mower blades; round and round the old homesite, head bowed and eyes picking up on every mined jewel of ancient broken glass, black boils of fire ants, white sand mounds of gopher holes, and hairy spirals of coyote scat. The armpit odor of gnarled red fungus, and the rooty smell of rich earth bursts. A startling explosion of quail making him snatch forward. Now and then glancing about to see if anybody is coming, if he is alone, and feeling the shoe in his pocket that could slip out at any time and blossom into evidence again. Should he bury it under the bricks in the well, should he bury it under the garbage in the overpass dumpster? On TV, it would be found regardless; on TV, the murderer would be found regardless.

❖ ❖ ❖

Round and round and looking down, ranging farther and farther from the old homesite, Roper begins to think he should have buried the shoe in the well with the body, which has remained miraculously undiscovered so far. But to go back now, he would be running a risk of Taylor or somebody coming up and catching him where he has no business being. He tucks the strings into the shoe, still driving, staring down at the spin of blond grass and tawny weeds for another shoe or sock or some object he can't imagine, and suddenly spies a coiled diamondback rattler like a gold rope chain in the mowed strip on his left. Head and tail raised, rattles shaking.

Out of habit, from his years working in the turpentine woods of Swanoochee County, Roper always keeps a snake stick handy. And out of instinct he now leaps from the tractor and takes the tobacco stick, stuck lengthwise between the seat and the housing, strolls over to the mad, whirring diamondback, and whacks it on the head till it lies writhing and braiding in the wet clumped thatch. When he is sure the snake is dead, he lifts it on the end of the stick and carries it dangling like a hot copper tube to the Isuzu, north of the old homesite. Dumping the snake to the bed of the pickup, he sees Math Taylor's white pickup spiriting in the rain up the pond road, center-field, and gets in and drives toward him, while sneaking the shoe from his pocket and tucking it beneath the truck seat. Not looking down because he knows Math Taylor has seen him and might be watching from inside his truck at the end of the pond road now.

When Roper gets close, Taylor steps from his truck and stands beside it, waiting in a green vinyl coat like Roper's. Roper pulls alongside, gets out, shuts the Isuzu door and starts toward the back.

"Didn't expect you'd be out here working in this rain," says Taylor, walking toward Roper.

"Got you a snake," Roper says—no better distraction than a rattler in this neck of the woods. In the quarters, Roper has seen deadly fights extinguished by the sur-prise sighting of a snake.

Taylor stands at the tailgate of the Isuzu with hands in the pockets of his coat just like Roper's and stares dull-eyed at the bright snake. Roper lifts it on the end of his stick and flips it to the wet road, diamonds flexing on the same sandy spot where Taylor's wife had died.

"Where'd you find him?" Taylor says without interest.

"Just a piece back thisaway from that old house yonder."

"He's about been denning under that stack of old tin, don't you reckon?"

"Yessir," says Roper, already regretting drawing atten-tion to the burial site, but knowing if he hadn't brought

the snake over, Taylor might have driven there, might
have found another shoe there.

"Soon as you get done mowing that side of the field,"
says Taylor, "why don't you go on and clean up that place.
It's a thousand wonders somebody didn't get snakebit
out there the other day. Bunch of junk for the most part.
I'm about done with saving stuff somebody's gone have
to tote off when I'm gone."

Does he mean leaving or dying? Roper wonders, feeling braver and meaner and more than ever innocent,
thinking about the search party missing the shoe and the
body. He looks close at Taylor's face—sick-sallow,
bloated, and old—which bears almost no resemblance to
the even-featured fiery young face of Math Taylor that
Roper calls up on occasion from the hate-fueled faces of
the mob thirty years ago on the Alapaha River bank, the
young face Roper still associates with the name Math
Taylor when he thinks the name.

Taylor is gazing all around, at the pond, at the pine
rows, at the old homesite, at the house with the green car
parked on the north side, as if looking for the woman
whose death had taken place under the very soles of his
hardened brown work boots.

"Mr. Math," says Roper, "I hate to tell you this."

"What, Roper?"

"I need a little ahead on what you owing me—maybe
twenty dollars if you can let me have it. I promise them
boys I take em to the fair."

"I forgot to pay you, Roper, I'm sorry." Taylor begins
fishing in his jeans pocket, frowning but not at Roper.
"Got this other on my mind, you know."

"I shore be sorry, Mr. Math," says Roper and takes the

three twenty-dollar bills Taylor holds out to him. As always, about twenty more than Roper is worth.

"I reckon you're helping out your mama with her groceries and light bill and all."

"Yessir."

"Yep," says Math Taylor, aqua eyes roving over the old homesite, "go on and clean that place up, whatever needs doing. I'll come over there once you start, if I'm here, and tell you what's good and what ain't. Wife was always after me for junking up the place."

A jangling sound erupts from inside the white truck, then another, and Taylor strides over, yanks open the door, and sits with one long blue denim-cased leg out in the rain, talking—"Yeah ... yeah ... uh huh ... I hear you!"—into the receiver of a cellular phone. He slams it down on its cradle, gets out and strides back to Roper and the gift snake.

"Got me a truck phone," says Taylor, unwrapping a stick of Red Man gum and offering one to Roper. "Driving me crazy, but not half as crazy as setting at the house, waiting. Bunch of fucking nuts out there ain't got nothing better to do."

He stops talking suddenly, chewing gum, starts to drop the gum wrapper but clenches it in his great fist, rain or tears rolling down his puffy face. Watching the renewed writhing of the snake with its smashed head.

❖ ❖ ❖

Roper eats from the plastic container of tallowy cold beef stew that his mama has sent to Taylor, then mows straight through the afternoon, straight into the evening, in the cold, slow rain, mowing slower and looking closer in the clumped wet thatch slung by the mower, keeping to his circle around the old homesite but growing more tense instead of less tense as the circle widens, dreading the time when he will get done mowing and have to start cleaning up. Though in his head the notion is brewing that he'll just quit work—an ongoing series of trips to see the man. If Math Taylor should ask. But if Roper quits working for Taylor now, he will be violating his probation. Math Taylor had given his word to the judge that he would work Roper Rackard if they would let him go. Roper moans, mowing into the rain blowing now from all directions, even after, judging by the distance he has mowed, he knows another shoe or sock cannot possibly be scattered so far from the old homesite. He has to make sure, has to make sure that no more evidence exists to link him to the crime that isn't a crime but is more and more taking on the characteristics of a crime.

Again, he is tempted to tell—had almost told Taylor when he took him the snake—and take his chances. On TV, the law or whoever would do an autopsy to determine the cause of death. One problem, according to TV, the longer Roper goes without telling, the more decomposed the body will become and the less chance there will be of determining the cause of death as a heart attack or whatever. And now Roper is stuck forever with a shoe to conceal like the truth.

Driving the tractor east across the field, toward his truck, he considers digging the body from beneath the bricks and taking it to the Taylor house, maybe leave it on Taylor's front porch. Before it gets too decomposed for an autopsy to reveal the cause of death. Putting the shoe back on the foot maybe.

But he hasn't fully appreciated the incriminating, maddening power of the shoe till he opens the truck door and spies one mildewed shoestring trailing on the floor mat from beneath the truck seat. He is so shook that he almost forgets about the chain Boss ordered, is looking right at the red chain snaked around the rafter of the tin shelter as he passes, headed out, and has to back the Isuzu up. He gets out without even considering whether anybody is watching and untangles the chain from the foot-adzed pole and tosses it into the bed of the truck. It collapses in a heap with linking shrieks that make Roper feel crazy.

❖ ❖ ❖

When he drives the Isuzu into Sweet's yard and spies his mama standing in the rain, Louise's side of the hedge, and Sweet standing in the rain, Sweet's side of the hedge, he knows they are fighting again. Louise, shrunk-wrapped in a clear plastic raincoat over black pants and white shirt, and Sweet, swelled up in oranger-when-wet tights and shirt, both bristling and shaking like the dogs circling and barking.

Roper turns off the truck and the babbling and barking pick up.

"What y'all be fussing bout now?" he says, getting out of the truck, locking the door, shoving through the hedge—Louise's side.

"This ole biddy here just jump on me for bad-mouthing Math Taylor," Sweet shouts, and begins marching along the hedge toward the road with her great breasts and rump jiggling, while Louise talks, while she talks, while Roper listens. Sweet: dazzling, hulking, with big teeth and hazel eyes bogged in a round brown face. Fake braid trailing down her thick back. "What I care if he cut his ole lady up and dump her in the deep freeze?" she says low, and Louise says loud, "Yo mouth be the ruination of this whole place," and follows Sweet along the hedge, with Roper and the sour-wet dogs following Louise along the hedge and stepping between Louise and Sweet when they start swapping swipes over the hedge. "Mama, you too old to be fighting," he says. Sweet slaps at Louise, misses, and slams Roper's left shoulder, and he stops and points at her house behind the bowed clothesline of twice-wet clothes. "Git on home, Sweet!" he yells, and she yells, "I am home!" and karate-kicks the door of the Isuzu with her calf-high brown suede boot. "Git this old ugly bunch of junk out of my yard, you sonofabitch, fore I call the law." Louise still jabbering and marching shoulder to shoulder with Sweet, back toward the rain-hissing chinaberry tree and away from the Isuzu, much to Roper's relief, switches to the hot topic of the boys taking up at Sweet's house. "Learning them boys all kind of trash," Louise says, and Sweet says, "They done know it, could learn me. Besides, what I want with some boy?" and eyeballs Roper as he heads toward his trailer door. "If I be wanting me a boy," she says and laughs, "I keep Roper there." Louise is jabbering loud, but can't out-jabber Sweet, till Louise starts mumbling, "Calling yo'self a divorce lawyer—folk ain't no more divorced than me."

"Cause yo old man be daid," shouts Sweet. "Think peoples don't know you have him kill. You and that . . ."

Roper opens the door, steps inside, and slams it hard to shut the sound.

6

Slow rain sets in for the rest of the work week, a blessing because Roper can stay home and guard the shoe inside the Isuzu and delay having to clean up the old homesite under Math Taylor's scrutiny. A curse too, because Roper is stuck in the quarters with nothing to do but dwell on whether Lora Taylor's body is right this very minute being uncovered from the well. Stuck with Bloop and Beanie slamming in and out of his trailer and begging for the truck keys and nagging him about the fair. Roper will take them on Friday night, he says, if they will go to school. Just stay away from Mr. Math's truck.

Friday morning, they go to school, leaving Roper in peace to mope and mull over his predicament in his dim, moldy trailer, or to battle the brats in his mama's overheated trailer in order to eat and catch snatches of TV news. The search for the missing woman is still on. Somebody claimed to have seen her in Orlando, Florida. A bum lead. It never fails to shock Roper when he sees the Taylor house and fields looking somehow shabbier and yet grander splashed on the off-hue screen of the slender portable.

In the kitchen, Louise talks to the TV through the children. "If Miss Lora be dead, it be the likes of Sweet what kill her with they mouth; it be her own kind what kill her with coldness. Poor lil ole lonesome thing." A child

coughs, coughs. "Here, take a swig of this cough medicine," Louise says, and while the children fuss and over-
turn drinks, and wander, she launches into the next
installment of her once-upon-a-time story about the
Freedom Riders in the sixties coming to the quarters—
eating fried chittlings at her table and using her outhouse—to get the blacks registered to vote. This time, it's
her fairy-tale version of a young white man signing up
with the Civil Defense, along with the rest of the local
white boys, in order to legally whip the blacks, but ending up using his authority to legally whip some whites
who he caught beating up on one of the local black boys.
She doesn't tell about the quarters burning, or about the
Freedom Riders' field trip into Never-Never Land, where
they tried to fit what they found into their fiction; or on a
broader scale, the sit-ins, the stand-ins, the bombings
and riotings, or about Lyndon Johnson's deception at
the National Democratic Convention in Atlantic City
that integrated blacks and whites on at least one score: a
mutual understanding that the truth is a lie. Neither
does she tell the children about Big Taylor escorting her
to the Swanoochee County courthouse in Cornerville to
register to vote. Roper wonders if the not-told stories are
forthcoming installments, or have already been told; he
wonders if she has omitted his name—the local black
boy—because she now considers Roper unworthy to be
paired with Little Taylor—the white hero.

The festive atmosphere in the quarters always picks up
on rainy days and as the weekends near. The music from
the juke louder, the jabbering louder, the activity on the
east curve luring Roper from the closed stale trailers
encircled by the circular hedge. As long as he is working,

he isn't tempted to wander, isn't tempted to hook up with his old buddies or seek out one of the women whose warm body in bed would make the slow rain cozy rather than dreary. But he has to guard the truck, and hope Sweet doesn't make good on her threat and call the law; he has to hang on to his money. Already he has given his mama twenty dollars to hold for his December fine installment; she fusses because he doesn't help pay for groceries. The man won't wait, he says. Them hungry boys won't either, she says.

Sweet's shack next door is alive with other women and men—drinking, fighting, loving. Even the dogs, including Roper's red cur bitch, congregate at Sweet's, where food scraps randomly get tossed out the door, and where, as Louise says, everybody but Sweet's four welfare children are welcome. Another reason the old woman has painted her windows black: Louise might have to hear what goes on at Sweet's house, but she doesn't have to see.

So far, Louise hasn't mentioned her run-in with Sweet, she hasn't even mentioned Lora Taylor to Roper again, and though he knows she has heard the report on the twelve-o'clock news, she acts as if she hasn't. Just sits in her spot on the ruptured green vinyl couch, overlooking the napping children curled like kittens on their pallets. She is wearing her own gray pants today, with a white shirt and holey white sweater, men's black shoes and white socks. Now and then Little Angel with cotton in her ears cries out or punches at her doll head, then sucks her thumb vigorously till her long lashes shutter her scuppernong eyes. Louise gets up and kneels beside her, rubbing her back and crooning in that mannish voice—"Wait in the waters, wait in the waters, wait in the waters . . ."

Roper hopes she will shut up soon, he hopes the Lora Taylor news updates are over for the day, if his mama is going to keep watching TV with him. Makes him feel like he does when people get riled and talk dirty on the talk shows, Louise taking it all in, unriled, but knowing Roper is riled.

The gas space heater hisses, a clock ticks, a public notice band unreels across the TV screen—REMEMBER 1996 IS ELECTION YEAR. REGISTER TO VOTE—in black and white.

"I done try that," says Roper to the TV.

And Louise to the TV: "Once," she says low, still on her knees, "thirty some-odd year ago. Wait in the waters, wait in the waters . . ."

"Like to get my head busted open trying."

"Wadn't for Little Taylor, you wouldn't *have* no head."

He shoves up from the chair, steps to the door, and opens it to let in the solemn rainy light. And when he looks back, she is sitting on the couch again.

"Big Taylor be a *fool* about that boy," she says, "have him riding round with him everwhere he go before he die. Little Taylor standing in that truck seat to see out when he be little bitty, then setting in the same spot when he get big."

"I hear that story a dozen times, Mama."

"Then hear it again." She plants both black shoes solid on the floor and props her elbows on her knees, burry gray head resting in her hands—her worrying position. "What gone come of Little Taylor?"

"I don't know, Mama. He'll about over it."

"You need to . . . you need to make Bloop and Beanie go to church with me."

"Why, Mama? So they can learn about salvation being free or freedom being free?"

"They ain't got nothing to remember by, to care about or be proud about."

"And we do?"

❖ ❖ ❖

By noon the rain has stopped. Cold air begins seeping into Louise's patched-up trailer. Roper could go to work now, could work the rest of the afternoon. But by the same token he doesn't have to, and doesn't have to go tomorrow, because he has seldom been known to work Saturdays, and reasons every day he can get by without working is one day more he delays having to start cleaning up the old homesite. Maybe if Roper delays long enough, Math Taylor will forget about the job or lose interest, just as he has seemed to forget or lose interest in farming the land behind his house since he started his construction business. Roper has never seen Taylor or anybody else even fishing in the pond, and he wonders if Taylor or anybody else knows about the old well.

As much as Roper detests having the boys around, when the school bus brings them home that afternoon he is glad for their on-the-spot, live racket. Wearing shorts, T-shirts, and jackets, they gobble up in ten minutes the food their grandmother spent the entire morning cooking—lima beans and rice and biscuits, and biscuit pudding from yesterday's biscuit batch.

Roper steps outside the door, to check on the truck parked in Sweet's yard, for one thing, and listens to his mama scolding the boys about wearing shorts in winter. Them babbling back about her being old-fashioned. Not too old-fashioned to cook for them, though.

It drives Roper crazy the way they treat his mama, who he had treated the same way when he was their age and sometimes still does. Different: Roper has a right; he is her real son.

"Hey, Roper," yells Bloop out the door, "don't you get off now and not take us to the fair."

"We gone to school, right?" Beanie calls from his spot before the TV.

"You boys gone be the death of me," says Louise, "tracking in that mud out of the yard."

"You one ticky old lady," says Bloop.

Roper knows she is just as glad as he is to have somebody to break the noxious spell of gas heat and TV soaps. He walks to the hedge between Sweet's yard and his mama's for a closer look at the truck. Locked tight with the white shoe under the seat.

Inside Sweet's house, a quarrel is going on—two men who sound like Walleyed Willie and Boss—then sounds of scuffling and Sweet scolding. A hard slam against the front wall, rocking the unpainted square shack, with dogs scratching on the half porch, bothered only by the fleas they swap.

Slipping through the hedge, Roper gets into the Isuzu and starts the engine, backs out with the left side scrubbing bushes, straightens up on the white clay road blighted by papers, bottles, and cola cans, and heads toward the highway, with yipping dogs drawing to the truck wheels like hummingbirds to red. Between the cluster of houses and the highway, the road has been scraped away till the shoulders of wheat broomsage and toasted dog fennels rise up on carved platforms of earth, revealing naked layers—white gumbo, red clay, and rich black dirt—like sample slices of time. A funnel for the rain sluicing from the swampy woods. At the highway, Roper turns left, climbing the railroad overpass, then right at the gravel road, where three green metal dumpsters sit beneath leached turkey oaks and magnolias.

His red cur dog has followed the Isuzu, and before Roper even brakes on the curb of dumpsters, the dog climbs like a goat to the top of a trash heap and noses beneath a square of rotting plywood. Water droplets tick from the claw leaves of the turkey oaks to the waxy leaves of the magnolias, to the fester of plastic bags and cardboard oozing over the sides of the dumpsters. Sound of peace, vision of plenty. A brown plaid couch to match Roper's doorside chair, which will stay forever to remind him of his sloth for not picking the couch up before the rain last summer; a mattress slumped against the center oak trunk and around it sodden newspapers and Gatorade jugs; a broken, puffy-skinned wood cabinet sinking into the oily earth; and a collapsed wheelchair, which means somebody, somewhere, is either better now or dead.

Always something new in and around the dumpsters, and always something old, stuff picked over by Roper and somebody else, who Roper is yet to lay eyes on during his daily dumpster forays. Usually Roper doesn't care who the other junk man is, because Roper beats him to the fresh trash each day and picks out what's most valuable—aluminum cans were bringing ten cents a pound last time Roper sold.

Now Roper does care about the other junk man,

because if Roper deposits Lora Taylor's running shoe in the dumpster, the other man might discover it. And though the probability of Junk Man Number Two making the shoe's connection with the missing woman is almost zero, Roper can't risk the shoe showing up somewhere else, either on some woman's foot in the quarters or as an object for some dog to gnaw.

Suddenly Roper realizes he is standing beside the truck, hefting the shoe in both hands like a precious glass dish, while a green car slow-motors past the dumpster; and before he can rethink, he tosses the shoe to the floor of the truck and slams the door, leaning against it. After the car has faded along the curve of the side road, he heads for the wheelchair to take home to Louise. The spoked chrome wheels are muddy and stuck. He carries it to the Isuzu anyway and places it in the oily truck bed, gets into the cab, and stuffs the shoe under the seat again. He'll just have to throw it out somewhere else, and spends all evening in the gelled cold of the Isuzu trying to find that perfect somewhere, while in the rearview mirror he checks for signs of the man, who might catch him driving. Roper is getting too brave.

Needing to rest, needing to think, needing to just be, Roper turns down the bumpy dirt lane to his grandpa's old house, south of the quarters. The three-path buggy road is almost grown up with evergreen myrtle bushes and scrub oaks and frost-charred goatspurs. Wet branches and bushes scrape the sides and underneath the Isuzu and send off screeches that make Roper's teeth clamp down.

In front of the rotting red house with its broken green porch banisters, Roper stops in the circular sand clearing, surrounded by pines and sweetgums, and listens to the close ticking of rain through the trees and the far-off shouts and laughter drifting on the north wind from the quarters across the railroad tracks. And in the west, distant thunder under clear, cold skies—either an airplane or the six-o'clock freight train out of Valdosta.

Roper opens the door, gets out, and fishes the shoe from beneath the seat, then heads across the rain-packed sand toward the thick woods, where the sun sparkles like fire on red maple leaves and water droplets linger on the tips of green pine needles. Smells of hydrated bark mold and chilling mud. Slapping at bamboos and branches with the shoe, cold blooming in slanted shadows, he locates the path he and his mama used to take from the quarters to Pappy's house. Long ago—not important.

Running now and breathing hard, he can smell the sharp creosote of the crossties before he reaches the railroad right-of-way, and stops short of the mowed embankment, and from a copse of myrtle bushes he sights west up the joints of rails to where the tracks vee out into the fiery disk of sun and forever.

No train yet. Nothing between him and the sun and the ends of the earth but the railroad overpass and its bowed shadow. No sounds but the lonesome clicking of grasshoppers in the cropped brown weeds and singed grass along the tracks. That and the rain ticking like a tightly wound clock in the woods behind and ahead.

Then a few yards east, across the tracks, bushes rattle, stunted trees shed great drops of rain, and out pop Bloop and Beanie. Bloop is wielding an old crowbar. Roper squats behind the myrtle bushes and watches their white running shoes climb the far slope to the flat railbed. Up and down the tracks, right past Roper, they wander in their khaki shorts, white caps, and white T-shirts with alien messages, peering down at the crossties.

"Just hope ain't no carload of fucking Fords," says Bloop, gazing up the tracks with his teeth shining and turns his cap bill to the back of his scrawny neck. Still walking, with the crowbar down like a divining rod seeking water.

"Hope ain't no nother load of diapers and dishes, what I hope," says Beanie, stooping and looking, then straightening up again. "After me a Vette, what I'm after."

Bloop pries up on a spike with the crowbar, not twenty-five feet from Roper's squatting place. He bends down and picks up the spike, stands and hurls it toward Roper's myrtle-bush hideout, where it drives into the loamy dirt at his feet.

Down the tracks, mumbling, they go, clunky white shoes short-stepping crosstie to crosstie, crunching in the sun-glinting gravel, till Bloop spots another spike, pries up on it with the crowbar, and commands Beanie to pluck it up and pitch it into the line of trees, other side of the track. Then back through the woods the way they came, bushes rattling, stunted trees shedding great drops of rain.

Eyes fixed on the scraggly sweetgum where the last spike has landed, other side of the tracks, Roper stuffs the shoe into the waist of his pants like a pistol, picks up the spike driven into the dirt at his feet, and starts up the slope to the tracks and down the other side to the spot where the last spike landed. He has to search around in the bushes for the spike, but finds it and starts up the embankment to the railbed again when he spies another spike in the brush on his right. Then another and another, all the way down an entire section of rails. Both sides.

Hurrying now, because he thinks he hears the train rumbling east, he begins tamping one spike and then another with a jagged rock into the rusty tie plates extending from the rails to the crossties. Four holes to each tie plate and only a couple of spikes for each.

In the violet afterlight of sundown, Roper stands listening to the whistle and rumble of the train and watches it trundle slow but steady along the tracks, over the joint of repaired rails and on. He watches the open cars of dull red, yellow, and blue rock by, but doesn't dash up and toss the shoe into one of the cars as planned, because he figures the boys could just as well have removed more spikes anywhere up and down the tracks, and with Roper's luck the next derailment of Pampers and Melmac dish sets, along with the shoe, could land in the law's lap.

❖ ❖ ❖

With the truck radio charging his senses with rap music, Roper drives along the back roads to Valdosta, while the boys rap with the speedy rapper and fuss about Roper driving too slow. How much money does he have for them to spend? How much farther? Where the hell are they anyway? A dirt road that cuts across Grand Bay Road to 84, Roper hopes. Hating himself for getting talked into taking them to Valdosta, home base for the man. First time he has driven to Valdosta since his drug trouble. If Math Taylor comes by the quarters and finds that Roper is gone in the truck, Roper might be sent back to jail.

A couple more jogs through the dark pinewoods and Roper hits 84, west toward Valdosta, with the boys revved up by the rapper and knocking about the truck, picking their hair before the rearview mirror while Roper's eyes shift from the left side mirror to the open highway. Swift automobiles overtaking the slow Isuzu, lights blowing up the inside of the truck, the boys' feverish tawny faces and glittery black hair. The stifling scent of body-warmed cologne, like some magic potion turning the work truck into a funeral limousine.

Roper steers the Isuzu off of 84 onto the grassed two-path entrance to the fairgrounds parking lot, where what seem like hundreds of cars and trucks are parked before the sweep of colorful carnival lights. Sound of hawkers and squealing girls and music. Two Ferris wheels reeling in the cold sky with a red-lit rocket like alien aircraft. Following the hand-held-flashlight motions of a police-man, who makes Roper's right foot want to bear down, Roper eases the Isuzu into the nearest empty parking slot, and hasn't cut off the engine before the boys spring out of the truck, hands stuck through the door for money. Roper doles out a twenty-dollar bill to each and watches as they lope-walk toward the ticket gate and dis-appear into the crowd along the sawdust path to the main building, gray cinderblock with khaki awnings and tents on the left side.

Quiet now, except for other cars and trucks pulling in alongside and behind the Isuzu, forming rows on the formless grass lot. Roper sinks back in the seat with his hands in his jacket pockets and watches the Ferris wheels turn in the milky city sky, the rocket spin, adults walking and children skipping between parked automobiles, laughing and talking, and considers the shoe under his seat, like an egg he's trying to hatch, which he could easily place beneath the blue Buick on his left as soon as the policeman moves another row south to park the incoming traffic raping Roper's peace with their engine racket, exhaust fumes, and headlights. All Roper would have to do is slip the shoe into his zipped jacket and get out and walk with the crowd and drop it and keep walking. So easy. So tempting, it makes him feel warm in the freezing truck. So terrifying that he waits till the warm feeling turns to cold dozing and he misses his chance.

The boys are back and the row where the Isuzu sits is almost empty. They slap the hood, then swing into the breath-warmed truck, bringing with them cold and the smell of cold. Hotdogs in one hand and Cokes in the other now, they fuss because they have run out of money, and if they had come on Saturday night—Midnight Madness—instead of Friday, they could have bought tickets for more rides with their measly twenty dollars; they could have stayed all night.

Roper starts the Isuzu and eases toward the highway exit, saluting the policeman with the flashlight—"the fuzz," as Bloop calls him. Almost free now, almost out of town, augering down the same dirt roads that had brought them, and safe again. Roper's eyes burn from the heater turned full blast because the boys in shorts are still freezing. Still fussing about Midnight Madness and trying to sweet-talk Roper into bringing them back on Saturday. He doesn't answer.

Beanie, in the middle, is holding a tiny stuffed dog he

won pitching dimes at tiers of dinner plates, that and a short woven straw tube to stick your fingers into and try to snatch them free without disjointing your knuckles. Which he does over and again, elbowing Roper, who is hellbent on getting back to the quarters, while watching in the rearview mirror for the man.

One last elbowing of Roper's sore ribs and one last jabbing of Bloop's flapping jaw, and the tube pitches to the floor under Roper's feet. Beanie reaches down and begins fishing for the tube, finds it, and sits up, holding the tube and one lace of Lora Taylor's white shoe. Which might be overlooked and forgotten if not for Roper snatching the shoe back and stuffing it under the seat, leaving the truck to roll where it will, which happens to be in the right ditch, jouncing them together, knocking heads against heads, and heads against glass, and coming to a hard-driving stop at a weedy culvert. Boys yelping and cursing and accusing Roper of trying to kill them.

Roper can see that the lip of the Isuzu hood has curled and figures he's driven the grill into the radiator, figures the jig is up, and feels almost relieved, ready to confess to driving the truck to town, ready to confess to murder if that's what it takes. Instead he backs along the ditch, surprised and a little disappointed that the truck will still go, and disappointed that he is once again in motion, once again into his weeklong pattern of trying to battle the beast that will end up eating him anyway.

7

Roper is amazed how good he feels the next morning with no sleep. How clear his mind, how sharp the images before his eyes, which he hadn't known were dull and weighted till now. He is glad it is over—almost over.

A note on the windshield, clamped under one of the wipers, reads: GOT A MAN NEED A 12 VOTE BATTRY. Roper crumples it in one hand and drops it to the dirt.

Even the quarters' dogs are sleeping when he sets out for the Taylor place in the wrecked Isuzu—only a bent bumper and grill. Sun strong through the spidered glass on the other side, where Bloop's head had struck when they hit the culvert coming home from the fair. No damage to the head except to loosen hard cussing.

Driving slow up the highway, Roper feels light, floating in the battered Isuzu like a boat on water. Gravel close under his feet, a slight brattling, cold pines and scrub oaks still, even the moss in the live oaks at the Taylor house hanging solid as wrought iron. Mowed fields white with frost and ruches of rust—robins skating and pecking. The house dead, the green car and white pickup parked on the north side, ice-crazed, frozen as if time has stopped.

But Roper is having to remind himself to breathe.

He pulls up to the front, before the quiet house, where the porch usually greenhousy with ferns is bare. The porch swing still, a mingled-gray cat sleeping in it. Roper gets out, starts to take the shoe from beneath the seat, but decides to tell first. At the porch edge he knocks on the gray floor cobbled with leather-brown oak leaves— even the wooden bench and rocker seats are padded with leaves—and stands back to wait. Listening to the sore-throated cawing of crows in the pecan trees behind the house. No sound inside the house till the cat uncurls and slinks from the swing, setting it swaying. The chains screak. The floor inside screaks. Footsteps sounding from back to front of the house. A head in the double window of the kitchen peering out.

Before Taylor had opened the door and stood holding it, before he had stepped out on the porch and walked sock-footed to the doorsteps, Roper had known exactly what he would say, had shaped the words in his head, but then they dissolved.

"What about it, Roper?" says Taylor, stale and sleepy-eyed, gray-blond curls massed in contrast with his naked crown. A stranger without his cap. Nobody Roper has ever known.

"I bring your truck home," says Roper, looking off at the Isuzu, at the oaks for proof that he is at the right place.

"What you mean *bring my truck home?*"

"You a good man, Mr. Math, always been good to me. Ain't never done nothing but right by me."

"You in some kind of trouble, Roper?" Taylor pockets his hands in his wear-softened blue jeans. Hair on his thick back and chest is matted under his white T-shirt, like sacked grass.

"Yessir," says Roper, "you might say that."

"You get caught driving?"

"Nosir, not yet."

"Somebody steal the gas out of the Isuzu again?" Taylor looks cold, sounds suddenly impatient. "Well, what then?"

"Wellsir, what I done was take them boys to the fair last night, and on the way home run your truck off in a ditch." Roper starts his tuneless whistling. Reflex.

A breeze lifts the moss in the oaks, signaling south, rain likely by Monday.

Long white-socked feet curving over the doorsteps, Taylor steps out to the caving brick walk and strides toward the front of the pickup. "Bent it up pretty good, didn't it?"

"Pretty bad," says Roper, following Taylor, whistling, bypassing him and heading for the other side of the Isuzu to get the shoe. But when he opens the door, his right hand reaches for the hood latch under the dash instead.

Taylor has to pry the hood up with his fingers to unstick it. Pokes his head inside. "Don't look like no damage to the radiator."

"Nosir, don't," says Roper, stepping around and peering under the hood with Taylor. "Cracked the side glass though."

"Anybody get hurt?"

"Nosir. Biggest boy got his head bumped's all."

"Well," says Taylor, walking on the sides of his socks around a patch of horny acorns, "ain't no harm done. Old truck ain't worth fifty dollars any way you cut it. Just see you don't be driving off nowheres but around here. Hate to see you get in trouble again."

"Yessir," says Roper, watching Taylor limp back toward the porch, heavy-haunched in his slept-in jeans.

"You mowing this morning," Taylor says, "or what?"

"Nosir, I gotta go see the man this morning." The minute Roper says it he figures he has messed up, because on Monday he has to go see the man for real. But one thing he knows now: Taylor doesn't suspect him of killing his wife, because Taylor doesn't consider Roper capable of killing, doesn't consider Roper at all. And another thing Roper knows: dead is dead and telling won't change that fact for Taylor or his wife, just for Roper.

❖ ❖ ❖

It should have been over then, after Roper had decided that telling would hurt rather than help, but as with everything else in his life, there is always somebody standing ready to trip him up.

This time it is his boys.

Roper has just lain down for an afternoon nap when they come rapping on his door. He can tell it is them by the mocking rhythm of their knocks: shave-and-a-hair-cut—two-bits. That kind of foolishness.

"Y'all go on now," he calls from his bed.

"We gotta talk," says Bloop.

"I talk to y'all when I get up, I'm sleeping."

"You gone take us to Midnight Madness?"

"I done take y'all to the fair last night, now go on."

"You gone take us tonight too."

"I say, go on."

"Got that missing lady shoe right here in my hand." Beanie. Sniggering.

Roper springs up, skating in his socks from the bedroom to the living room to the front door. When he opens it, Bloop is propped against the jamb with his right elbow, chin resting on his fist.

"April fool," he says.

Beanie peeps around him, grinning with his gapped top teeth shining.

"What that you say bout that shoe?" says Roper, blocking the doorway.

"You kill her, didn't you?" says Bloop.

"You crazy, both of y'all." Roper backs to the chair by the door, sits, and stares at the floor. Two sets of clunky white running shoes fill the rust-flecked tile squares.

"What you do with the body?" says Bloop.

"Ain't do nothing with no body," says Roper.

"Man!" says Beanie, walking, plopping on the nest of clothes along the west wall. "I can't picture you messing up nobody. Granmama gone kill you."

"I say I ain't do nothing, now git on out from here." Roper stands up, balling his fists, and nods toward the open door.

"We going, man," says Bloop and swings out the door. "Come on, Beanie, let's go see can't we find somebody want to hear bout that shoe."

"Get back in here," says Roper, and Bloop backs to the door, backs through the door, and stands grinning and staring out with his left hand presented to Roper.

"Give us the key to that Zuzu, man." Bloop snaps his fingers.

"Can't give you that key, boy," says Roper. "Do and I'm dead."

"Mr. Math ain't studying you," says Beanie, standing, walking, stopping behind Bloop.

"I know that," says Roper.

"You can take us, though, can't you?" says Bloop.

"Ain't got no money for y'all nohow." Roper watches the two sets of white running shoes line up, heels to toes.

"But you can get some," says Beanie. "Mr. Math let you have some."

"He done pay me up."

"He give you some toward next week then."

"Hey!" Roper shouts, shooting to his feet. "I can't go begging money off that man."

"I bet you better," says Bloop, walking. Both sets of shoes walking.

❖ ❖ ❖

Roper only asks Taylor for twenty, for the man. With a promise to be on the Taylor place mowing Monday afternoon. No mention of cleaning up the old homesite, which he feels sure Taylor has lost interest in anyway. Taylor only asks Roper not to drive the Isuzu to town, that's all.

But this time Taylor seems put out for sure, having Roper show up twice in one day. Taylor is dressed in a rough-dried maroon shirt that makes his ruddy face blaze, brown belt tugged tight on his round paunch.

"They got me flying down yonder to Miami this time, look at another body could be my wife's." Taylor has one work boot inside the white Chevy pickup; an alarm is dinging, dinging, dinging, till he yanks the key from the ignition. "Aggravating sonofabitch!" he says and sits, sorting through papers on the dash.

Roper doesn't know whether Taylor is cursing the dinging or the law or him.

"Won't be good news," says Taylor, "no matter what. Beginning to look like she just fell in a hole somewhere. About like her."

"Yessir," says Roper.

"I wish you'd quit that," Taylor snaps, staring suddenly at him. "I told you a million times to quit saying *sir* to me; you don't understand . . . me and you . . . How old are you?"

"Fifty-four, last May."

"Well, that makes me about a year older than you," Taylor shouts, "which don't make me your sir." His face is like a red balloon about to pop. "And while you're at it, work on not calling me Mr. Math either. Call me Little Taylor, like Mama Lou, call me Jack the Ripper, like everybody else. Call me Buddy, like you used to before they beat the shit out of you." He grabs hold of the steering wheel, swings his other leg inside, and says low, "Okay?"

Roper almost says "Yessir" again.

He would like to go now, needs to go now. Doesn't know how. Just steps onto a humped oak root in the flocked leaf shadows of the great oak, north side of the house.

"Next thing you know the law'll be back to blaming me," says Taylor and starts the white pickup. Closes the door and backs from the sideyard as if Roper isn't on the place.

Roper watches him leave, then gets into the Isuzu and drives around the house to the tin shelter. Four identical black batteries sit solid in the dust along the tin wall, and Roper picks one up by its cable handle and lugs it to the Isuzu. One less order to fill on Boss's Christmas list.

❖ ❖ ❖

On the way home, Roper again starts figuring how to get rid of the shoe, though he imagines, now that the boys have guessed, he is doomed anyway. He might as well keep riding it around, he decides, after pulling down a woods road and stopping before a thicket of fanned palmettos and wax-berry myrtle bushes. A good enough place to hide the shoe, except for deer hounds barking all around, which means hunters are in the area and might have been watching from deer stands in the tall pines with the wind whistling over Roper's head. Besides he just cannot bring himself to get rid of it—his only hold on evidence that might lead to him. The body is buried and he is certain there is no other evidence to point to the fact that the body is close to home. He will slip the shoe out of the Isuzu when he gets to his trailer and hide it inside till he can bear to part with it.

But when he gets home and begins searching beneath the seat for the shoe, it isn't there. He gets out, kneeling on the dirt beside the Isuzu, and searches for it among grease rags and bottles and cans and a black comb with broken teeth.

He springs up, spying his mama in the dark doorway of her trailer, and walks toward his own. "Tell them boys I say come over here when they get ready to go to the fair," he says.

"They ain't here," she says.

"They at Ahab's?" he says.

"Might could be," she says and vanishes like a Halloween spook from the doorway.

When he opens the door to his trailer, he sees them sitting against the facing wall, bare brown knees up and hands behind, like hostages.

"Where the shoe at?" Roper says. "How y'all get it out of that truck?"

"Ain't seen no shoe," says Bloop. "You, Beanie?"

"What shoe?"

"Ain't taking y'all to no fair till somebody hand over that shoe."

"Man, we ain't got no shoe." Beanie scoots from the wall and holds out both hands, tawny palms flipping to brown topsides.

Roper eyeballs Bloop and walks toward him. Bloop rolls his eyes, grinning, and holds out his hands too, gets up and bounce-walks in a circle to show that the shoe isn't behind him. Roper's eyes shift to Beanie, and Beanie gets up and walks in a circle like Bloop. Both humming and waltzing about the room.

A train suddenly wracks the trailer with rumbling and vibration, and Roper waits for it to pass.

"Okay," he says, "what you want now?"

"Just Midnight Madness," says Bloop. "For now."

"Then what?"

"We let you know."

"I tell you what," says Roper, "for two boys picking at a killer, y'all mighty brave."

"So you did kill her?" Bloop.

"I ain't kill nobody. I just say . . ."

"What you use on her?" says Beanie.

"I done tole you I ain't. . . . Y'all better come up with a shoe."

"We done give it to somebody for safekeeping," says Beanie.

"In case something happen to us," adds Bloop.

"You see that trash on the TV," says Roper.

"You don't know though, do you?"

"Load up in the truck," says Roper.

"Huh uh," says Bloop, bounce-walking toward the door, "we done change our mind. Give us the key to that Zuzu."

8

As much as Roper had hoped his mama wouldn't ask why he'd let the boys take Taylor's truck over the weekend, he now wishes she would ask. He wishes she would ask just the right question to make his head tip and spill the whole mess through his mouth. Though everybody says she is crazy, and Roper agrees she is a bit on the strange side, he still believes in her power to fix messes. And too, he'd like to know what she is thinking, why this sudden pouty silence. On the long ride to Valdosta, Monday morning, to see the man, Roper even tries to bait her into talking by telling her that Mr. Math had to fly in an airplane to Miami to look at another dead woman's body. She says, "I seen that," meaning she has seen it on the TV news. Then nothing more till she says, "Don't look like you all that up-in-the-air over where it be her or not."

Little Angel somersaults over the seat between them, and scoots close to Louise and gazes at Roper like he's the boogerman. In the backseat, the other children scramble and grumble—ain't fair, Little Angel getting to sit up front. Louise just sits mum and fuming behind the steering wheel of the chugging station wagon. Her hair is standing in wiry tufts, like worn steel wool, makes her look madder, meaner. Her plum-tree switch is on the split blue vinyl dash. Her square jaw throbs. Not a good sign.

Roper stares ahead, up the gravel highway and each side, at the pine trees rocking in the wind, at ribby cattle huddling in a windswept pasture, at the gray clouds scudding out of the west—Peter's Mudhole. By noon it will be raining, and Roper won't be able to mow for Taylor today, and if he had any money he would for sure catch the Trailways bus this time, he would for sure walk straight out the exit door of the probation office and never be seen again. One problem with that thinking is, the mess won't end with Roper never being seen again—somebody will tail him, maybe even the man. And two, Roper will never be able to go somewhere he cannot imagine, which he cannot imagine because he's never been.

He is doomed anyway. Why run?

All day Sunday, while the boys drove the Isuzu around on stolen gas, Roper had tried to come up with a solution to the mess: how to get the shoe back from the boys, how to keep from having to clean up the old homesite with Taylor—Roper no longer thinks about telling Taylor the truth. The mess he dwells on fixing dates only from last Saturday when the boys stole the shoe. But mostly what Roper had done on Sunday was backtrack over how he'd practically confessed to murdering a woman he hadn't murdered and what he should have said to the boys instead.

Well, what is done is done. He is doomed.

In the probation-office waiting room, while he waits for the man to call him in, Roper sits in one of the orange plastic chairs along the front wall and listens to the skinny woman with pudgy boneless hands at the desk ahead talking to somebody on the telephone about the weather: a tornado watch is in effect till seven P.M. Ah, so that's what's wrong with Mama—worried about the weather. Roper won't mention the watch to his mama, who has become suspicious of every cloud since tornadoes started targeting mobile homes—so says the TV. Just as she is suspicious of every stranger in the quarters, who might be a dope dealer or a child molester. She is forever going to her door, looking out for clouds and strangers, and yet has painted her windows black to keep from seeing. Proof she is crazy. Was it the Freedom Riders made her crazy, or the children, or TV?

Roper's probation officer, in dove gabardine slacks geared tight on his bloated waist, opens the door behind the receptionist's desk, strolls over and slaps a manila folder on top, and without even looking at Roper says, "Rackard, you can come on in."

Roper springs from the chair and follows the probation officer, wearing trim bedroom-type slippers that make him look sissy. But he is a big man, a tough man, talks rough. He used to be all that stood between Roper and jail—before Lora Taylor—but now seems to Roper as if he is only going through the motions, same as Math Taylor does. In the low white room, bare but for a heavy brown desk, two chairs, and one wall shelved with lives in manila folders, Roper sits in the chair before the desk of the officer, who rocks back in a swivel chair and hooks his hands behind his head. His graying brown hair is wrapped over his bald crown like a bandage.

"Still working for Math Taylor, I guess?" he says.

"Yessir, regular."

"Sure bad about his wife."

"Bad, sho nuf."

"Hear the Swanoochee County sheriff questioned you."

"Yessir."

"Wadn't no reason to suspect you, was there?"

"Nosir!" Roper laughs, wiggles, crosses his feet. "You know me—ain't never been in no trouble like that."

"Just drugs, right?"

"Nosir, I wadn't into that neither."

"They caught you with the dope at that juke out there at Withers."

"I was there, I just wadn't doing it."

"Well," the officer says, rising, "that's all water under the bridge, right? You straightening up now, right?"

"Yessir, trying to." On his way out of the office, Roper again edits what he has said. What he should have said. But he is doomed anyway.

❖ ❖ ❖

At the Taylor place that afternoon, Roper is glad to be back on the tractor, mowing into and away from the thought-stunning warm wind. The planted pines south of the old homesite dip and sway, and a sheet of tin flaps and shrieks on the stack in front of the crumbling old house. The same sheet of tin Roper had placed over the wellsite he has now made visible by mowing the cat-claw briers around it. Still a patch of plum whips, the brittle pear tree with its bent bare branches, and the mammoth pecan tree with tulip hulls of seedling nuts almost touching the low gray clouds. Then sudden rain pecking at Roper's face and slashing across the mowed fields, a rack of navy clouds scrolling from behind the west woodsline like a window shade shutting out light. Rushing of wind rising and silencing the *clat-a-clat-clat* of the tractor.

Roper had parked the Isuzu on the creek road in front

of the old homesite, and standing with his hand holding his cap, steers the tractor over the bumpy field toward the truck. Wind whipping at his jacket and pants and rain pricking his face like an ice pick. When he gets off the tractor and starts toward the truck, he has to strain against the wind to keep from being blown backward. Tries to run but is only walking, slow like uphill water. Pines on his right wringing, trunks scrubbing and groaning like timbers on a ship, some snapping like dog fennels. Lightning shattering the navy bowl of sky, and at the same time thunder, quaking the ground as if sky and earth have been riven at the seams.

Almost to the Isuzu, sitting solid in the wind-driven rain, but looking as if it is rolling away from Roper because of forward-sweeping saplings and weeds and sand storming up the two-path road. Lightning spears the ground on Roper's left, but he shoves on till he reaches the Isuzu, tugs open the door, and slips inside, and clutches the steering wheel like a race-car driver. Sounds of howling and rain on the metal roof give way to the pounding of hail, like machine-gun fire, then sudden silence. Sudden stillness and darkness. And just as sudden, hail again and thundering like a thousand jets with the truck rocking and the rain-streaming glass collecting russet pinestraw, green leaves and blond thatch, like metal shavings drawn to a magnet, till only peep spaces emit smothered light. And all around him the shrieking of tin and branches snapping and an end-all rumble and quake, and finally the cozy pecking of slow rain coming straight down. And light.

Roper opens the truck door to cold, piney air and cropped pines and folded tin decorating the taller black-gums in the woods on his left. It's as if the world has shifted and Roper and the Isuzu have been set down in some foreign place. Moss in pine trees, pine burrs in oaks. Navy rags from the old homesite flagging stubble across the field, as if Lora Taylor's body has been sucked from its bricked-in grave and scattered. A queer openness about the old homesite hill where the bight of the sky shows blue through trailing white clouds. The thick trunk of the pecan tree horizontal instead of vertical, as if the field has tilted, spiny branches spread over the space where the old house used to sit, which means, if Roper is thinking right, estimating right, in the blue cold light of the afterstorm, that the well is now and forever capped by the tree trunk.

Through the rain haze, Roper scans the broken landscape for the black vinyl roof of Taylor's house, spies it, spots the oaks in their usual place, one topless and leaning, and the tin shed in the pecan grove with tin peeled back. He gets into the Isuzu again, starts it, drives forward till he gets to the limb-blocked creek road, backs up and turns around and heads toward the house, searching through the rain for the white house. Brittle oak branches, some with orange hearts shining, lay scattered about the yard; two shutters have been ripped from the south windows; a porch chair sits in the middle of the oak island as if somebody has placed it there. The green car, plastered with greener leaves and ropes of moss, sits alone on the north side of the house, same as it has since its driver died from a heart attack or whatever.

Roper smiles, can't stop smiling, smiles even as he stops at the peeled-tin shelter to pick up a crescent wrench for Boss. Roper is still smiling when he gets back into the truck and drives through the field again and around the vacuum-cleaned old homesite to view from a different vantage the tree broadside of the well, its great trunk entombing the body forever and ever, amen. Now if he can just get hold of the shoe.

❖ ❖ ❖

That night Roper willingly hands the Isuzu key over to the boys and listens till the muttering of the engine clears the curve and whines up the highway. Then whistling, he makes a beeline for his mama's trailer to search for the shoe. No, he does not believe their story about passing the shoe on to somebody else for safekeeping. Who? Their grandmother? Even if she believed them, she wouldn't turn her own son over to the law if . . . well, even if he murdered somebody. Not Sweet either; they wouldn't have handed the shoe over to Sweet, who can't find her own shoes half the time. The shoe has to be hidden at Louise's.

When Roper steps into the living room of Louise's trailer, with a roll of clean clothes under his right arm, he sees her settled in on the ruptured green vinyl couch, watching TV. Pouty, ruminating—dressed in a wild red pantsuit with rhinestone-studded buttons—apparently focused on the sports news, which she cares nothing about, but waiting for the weather, which she does. If she has heard about the tornado this afternoon, she doesn't mention it.

"I come to bathe up," he says and traipses between her and the TV, so that she has to nod to see the next football play. Touchdown.

Lights on throughout the lengthwise trailer, and everywhere cardboard boxes of Mason jars and Jesus plaques, roach-specked letters from Annie-the-Freedom-Rider, old clothes and shoes and crocheted potholders. Hall growing up in junk, even a box of lead-tinted pots and pans salvaged from the cabin that burned in the sixties; same junk Louise and Roper had carted to and from the scorched cabin on the east curve—next door to Little Ahab's rising hovel juke—which she had moved into right after the fire because she refused to live at the big house with Math Taylor, and moved out of a few months later because, as she said, she would rather live in a tent on the hardroad than have the same sorry people who had lied about registering to vote, and who had gone to the dogs after Old Ahab got killed and Wainer Taylor died, tramping through her yard all hours. True enough about the dogs—they seemed to take over after the fire—itchy, prowling, multiplying like mice. But Roper suspected that Louise's harping about the voting business was an expression of something she couldn't name. All he knew was his mama had swapped off the conveniently placed cabin for the comforts of trailer living, which keeps her tuned in to the weather. Go figure it.

On Roper's left, her closet-sized bedroom, between the living room and the boys' bedroom, facing the mildew-gray bathroom with its rotting floor and blackened window. A faded doll in a ruffly yellow crocheted dress is propped on the pillow of her neat cot. And then the back room, the boys' room, the big room, but like the hall closing in with walls of stuff. Boy stuff. So much stuff in the musty room that at first Roper despairs of ever locating the shoe. But it has to be here. Lots of other shoes—where did they come from? Even tire tools under the boxy bed, new-looking and shiny behind the dingy draped sheet. Between the springs and the mattress, blue and green striped and new-looking too? No shoe. Lifting the mattress from foot to head, Roper finds only a porn magazine pressed open to a man having sex with a goat.

In the bulging closet, on the bottom shelf, Roper finds a pack of cigarette papers he knows are used for rolling marijuana, along with a roach clip and a precious-looking silver spoon and a couple of plastic Ziploc bags with crumbs of what looks like beeswax but can only be crack cocaine. Bright-colored butane lighters everywhere: in jacket pockets, jeans pockets, shorts pockets, in the nest of dirty clothes on the floor, delightful looking as a kid's Matchbox cars.

From the bedroom, Roper can hear the TV weather report and then the TV news—news of sex and drugs and crime—and listens for news of Lora Taylor and hears none and considers the irony of his mama painting her windows black and holing up inside her trailer to isolate herself from sex and drugs and crime. He stuffs all the drug stuff into his pockets, then lifts the mattress and takes the porn magazine and rolls it and sticks it into the roll of his clean shirt and pants.

Between layers of comic books and T-shirts, wall side of the bed, Roper thinks he has located the shoe, but it turns out to be an old scaly-white Reebok belonging to one of the boys when he was younger. He keeps searching till he hears his mama's mopey footsteps moving from living room to kitchen, hears water sluicing through pipes under the trailer, then slips from the boys' room to the hall to the bathroom; runs the shower a few minutes, turns it off, and walks out. Louise's red rump shows around the refrigerator door in the kitchen.

As he is leaving her trailer, it occurs to him that his mama had to know he was searching in the boys' room but hadn't wanted him to know she knew. Simpler like that.

❖ ❖ ❖

Under cover of the canopy chinaberry, north end of Roper's trailer, he reclines in one of the rain-soaked chairs, footrest up and headrest propped on the metal wall. Freezing. So cold he is tempted to go inside to wait for the boys, but warm with satisfaction. One hand blood-warmed, fingers sunk into the fur of the dozing red cur on his right. Each time Sweet's back or front door slams, the dog flinches, but settles again as Roper scratches its bumpy spine—ticks. Ticks like warts from head to tail. All quiet inside Louise's trailer, and if not for her windows painted black, Roper would suspect her of spying on him. But of course she is in bed by now, wrestling dream devils from the past where she belongs.

Roper twitches his toes to the music from the juke—a zippy song blurred by high volume. He has heard the music so loud for so long it's like his own heartbeat. Just as he has smelled the raw sewage from the surrounding houses so long it's like his own body odor. He might go to the juke tonight; this could be the night. Or, if he gets to feeling any better, his old-self feelings, he might go to Sweet's.

Across the sandy road, lit white by overhead security lights, the front wall of Lucy-the-big-assed-nurse's trailer is shadow-stenciled with a bamboo vine trailing from one of the light poles. A perfect peaceful picture, depicting calm. Roper could go there, though he never has before, at least not for what he goes to Sweet's for; but Lucy's long white Caddy is gone, meaning she is gone. Hot on the roads ever since she bought that new-used car.

An automobile slows on 129 and turns off the highway onto the quarters road, and Roper recognizes the sound of Dreamer's old rag-top rust Thunderbird—pinging whine to the engine. Headlights purge the shadows from the road, lighting up cans and bottles and paper and a blue five-gallon bucket belonging to Roper's junk collection, which he tries to keep contained within the circular hedge. The Thunderbird slow-motors past Roper's lookout, then on around the loop of the quarters, radio booming like drums in a marching band. The car stops at the shanty behind Louise's trailer and the drums go still, and Little Angel's croupy cough and the music from the juke fill in.

Dreamer: bony, lonesome, raspy as a metal file. Decipherer of dreams. Last summer she predicted that Roper would either kill somebody or be killed himself before the end of the next year. He had dreamed about the old days and hog killings—fresh meat. Well, he hasn't killed anybody yet and it is only two months till the end of 1995. The roots of his hair prickle, thinking about the other possibility.

A freight train rumbles east, quaking Roper's trailer and the headrest of the chair propped against the north wall. He closes his eyes, luxuriating in the vibrating chair, in the whistle and clack and roar that represent the rest of the world's being industrious, responsible, and on time.

When Roper looks again, the hundred-watt light on

Sweet's front porch shows her standing on the porch edge nearest his chair, holding a white Melmac bowl with a wheat motif. (Another thing all the households in the quarters have in common: at least one set of white Melmac dishes with wheat motifs.) Dazzling, hulking, sweet Sweet.

Sweet in sheeny pink tights and tunic sweater with gold snakes, that fake braid hanging down her back like a whip. Sweeter than a baby's first sugar tit, or a boy's first lollipop. Sugar substitute, what a young man graduates to, what he was born for. Those creamy, dimpled, plumb thighs, the sucking warmth tucked demurely between them. Cracker Jack prize.

She laughs out, a bull-like bellow, and Roper irons his back to the chair. Has she spotted him? Is she coming to whack off his penis for snubbing her because she sided with that woman on the TV news who whacked off her husband's penis? Then Roper spies two red-tipped cigarettes budding in the dark beyond the hedge, bodies and heads of Walleyed Willie and Boss ghosting into the eaves' shadow from Sweet's porch light. She rakes food from the bowl to the dirt, jangling spoon on plastic, and sudden cats and dogs slink and dart from the shadows, snatching scraps. Roper's red cur sits high, but bows her head as Roper strokes her.

"Not tonight," he says.

❖ ❖ ❖

Midnight and just about the time Roper has given up on the boys coming home, the Isuzu slews into Sweet's yard, close along the hedge, so close Roper can almost touch the driver's door through the twiggy branches. Roper waits till the headlights die and the doors open, then stands and leans over the hedge. Right at Bloop-the-driver's ear.

"How long you boys been doing dope?" Roper says low.

"Hey!" Bloop wheels, ducks—"Shit! Fuck!"—and Beanie on the other side dodges through the streaked light of Sweet's yard, heading for the road.

Bloop's toothy black face rises from behind the hedge like a bad egg in water. Facing Roper. "Man, what you mean doing that?" says Bloop to Roper, then hollers out to Beanie, "Ain't nobody but Roper."

Beanie doubles back with his fists balled in the pockets of his oversized khaki shorts, falling in line behind Bloop now showing around the end of the hedge, shoulders slumped, heads hung. Both of them. Sullenly they march on toward the door of their grandmama's dark trailer, around boils of Roper's festering junk. The bitch cur stands, stretches, and slinks their way, wagging her tail. Bloop kicks at the dog and loops back with Beanie keeping step, straight toward the chinaberry and Roper.

"What you mean scaring us like that?" Bloop says.

"I'm onto you, boys," says Roper, and pulls out the Ziploc bag of crack crumbs and shakes it. A faint rattle. "Ain't y'all thirsty?"

"Ain't none of our shit," says Beanie, sidling up to Bloop with his teeth chattering. Both of them.

"You been in our stuff," says Bloop. "Looking for that missing lady shoe, I bet."

"You get it right that time."

"Well, you ain't getting no shoe, don't matter what," says Bloop.

"Ain't nobody gone believe him nohow," says Beanie,

"not and him a fucking rockhead hisself." He laughs, jigs with his hands in his pockets. "Man, I'm bout to freeze my balls off standing around out here."

"Yeah," says Bloop. "Who gone believe you head of us?"

"Law might not believe me, but they be keeping a eye on who I sic em on."

"You be sicking em on yo buddies then."

"Willie and Boss, huh?"

"We just boys," says Bloop. "Law don't do nothing to boys."

"Pen's full of boys," says Roper.

"Then we tell em bout that woman you waste," says Beanie, jigging full circle to face Roper.

"I ain't waste no woman," says Roper. "Shoe ain't no proof nohow."

"Then how come you so fucking crazy to get it back?"

"Cause might look like I do it."

"Give us back our shit and we think about it," says Bloop.

"When you bring me the shoe, I give back your shit." Roper reaches behind him to the chair with his clothes roll and pulls out the porn mag and holds it up so that the light from Sweet's porch shines on the man and the goat. "Bet you Granmama like this," he says. "Member how she always be reading y'all that goat book when y'all little-bitty . . . what she call it?"

"*Heidi*," says Beanie with his arms pulled into the folds of his boxy white T-shirt.

"Uh huh," says Roper, "that the one. Have a little cripple girl go to live with her granpa—love goats."

"That was Claire—Claire the cripple girl," says Beanie. "Peter the one love goats."

"Hush up, Beanie," says Bloop, sucking his fat lips in. "He just messing with us."

"Yeah, Granmama gone love this one," says Roper and rolls up the magazine again.

"Man, you wouldn't show Granmama that," Beanie whispers loud. "She have a fucking heart attack."

"Mama getting old," says Roper, "gotta go somehow."

"Ain't that old," says Bloop.

"Besides, don't look like y'all all that worried about tattling on your old man. Do it?"

"Aw," says Beanie, "we's just pulling your leg, Roper." He starts circling again, nerved-up laughing. "You know that."

"I doubt it," says Roper. "I figger you two subject to do anything. Derailing trains, stealing gas, stealing money from your own grandma what raise you."

"Who tell you that shit?" says Bloop. "We ain't never take a dime off that old woman."

"Just get me the shoe," says Roper, making headway now. So he thinks.

"No lying, Roper, we ain't got it no more," says Beanie. "Granmama taken it from us and we can't lay hands on it nowhere."

BOOK TWO Louise

9

Louise would like to think that before she dies she has gotten Roper's attention with something other than a switch.

A shoe will do.

She pats her apron pocket, and the shoe rattles in its newspaper wrapping. She is slow-moving this morning, stove up from staying inside during the cold spat, Tuesday through Friday. The children are wild, as wild as the sunflower print pants she is wearing. They scamp across the sunny yard, making games of Roper's junk: somersaulting inside old tires, painting rainbows on the blue sky with spewed rainwater from cola bottles, trampolining on inner tubes. All except Little Angel, who is feverish with croup and kittenwalks, sucking her thumb, behind Louise. Saturday now and Roper is home from work, holed up in his trailer, maybe watching Louise creep toward the collard patch behind her trailer, where backyards merge in the eye of the quarters loop. Just one big smear of tramped dirt and weeds, hatching trash. She suspects Roper knows she has the shoe, because suddenly Bloop and Beanie are no longer gallivanting in the Isuzu, because all week Roper's been keeping to himself—probably starving, probably wondering what Louise intends to do with the shoe. Maybe even thinking that she won't do anything with the shoe, since so far she has failed to tell that on Halloween day he did go back to work after lunch.

She always knows what Roper and the boys are into or up to, and they always know she knows, but know she won't tell whomever she should tell; they have that kind of hold on her. But this time she will tell; that is, if Roper doesn't do the right thing and tell Math Taylor the truth first. No, she doesn't believe Roper killed Lora Taylor, but she does believe he knows more than he has told. It's been a while since she believed in justice for a black man, and she's still not sure she does, but she does believe in Jesus and the kind of suffering-with Jesus commanded, be it black, white, or red man. She's almost done waiting for Roper to feel such compassion for Math Taylor— plain old pity would do—who she had wet nursed next breast to Roper, which must make for some kind of bond between them, sharing the same milk, as well as blood. Another reason for telling, so many they gell in her head, but as much as anything she wants to see something end, the end of something.

In the collard patch, she sidles between rows, cropping the tough, filmy-green leaves and tucking them under one arm. Rich black dirt, from where her cabin burned in the sixties. Brittle gray boards and shingles that had witnessed her supple years—all ashes. Scabs of chimney bricks and shards of crock bowls, and even a bent, baked spoon she remembers from her old kitchen. Everyday reminders, little things that were big to Louise. A fine garden spot, though a sorry trade-off. At the end of the row, she stands and peers back at the children making use of Roper's useless junk, then down at Little Angel grafted to her right leg like a berrying vine. She has a head full of braids, bound in machine-gum colored beads. From this point Louise can see the entire quarters, oddly still, oddly quiet, except for the children laughing and squealing. She can see each trailer and shack and the white frame church on the south curve facing her backdoor neighbor Dreamer's house. Paper and bottles and tin cans bank along the hoop road. Ribby dogs sun on the dun dirt. And Louise would just as soon not see, but can look now without crying inside, because suddenly she can picture her place—seventy acres, left to her by Wainer Taylor—clean and orderly as it used to be, her people at last coming around, maybe even registering to vote. So much promise in one shoe.

But naming off each person in her head, inside those patched, buckling shacks and trailers, she can come up with only a few who might actually clean up or vote, and only a couple of old grannies or aunties who will help raise the children. Two, she tallies up two women, one of them her own self. No men. Scanning the houses, Godlike, she passes right over Sweet's house—woman won't never change—and on to Roper's rust trailer, and marks his door in her mind with lambs' blood. Somebody who will stand for something—one man— who will set an example for his boys, who will take over her people after she is gone. If old folks make it past the sharp turn of a season, Louise has noticed, they usually make it till the next. She will likely live at least till next spring.

Passing again through the yard strip between trailers, she sees Roper sunning on his concrete-block doorstep— slumped, eyeing the dirt, with elbows ditched on his knees, as if watching the industry of ants. She walks straight, spry, right past him, doesn't speak. He'll have to come to her. She will give him a week.

❖ ❖ ❖

Come noon, she has collards and hamhocks stewing in her stewpot, wafting a swampy odor throughout the trailer, and knows Roper can smell the greens and almost regrets having painted her windows black, because to check on the children outside, as well as her progress with Roper, she has to keep going to the open door. The children are still playing in the junk heap, except for a couple of the older ones—five years, going on fifteen— who are scrunched under the white table, sniggering, playing at what Louise has to believe is innocent play because she doesn't have time to check now, she doesn't have the mind set for a lesson on playing nice. Roper has left his sunning spot on the doorstep, but the blue Isuzu is still parked in Sweet's yard, and Louise soon hears him pacing inside his trailer.

Bloop and Beanie slip through the hedge between Sweet's shack and Roper's trailer, and slouch toward Louise's door. She steps inside, fanning houseflies with a dishrag on her way to the kitchen, and adds some water to the shrinking greens. Living room and kitchen, one long room. Doll-housy appliances on the south end, and trailer-flimsy chairs, table, and couch on the north end.

"Them boys know what from what," she says to herself. "Would eat my big toe if I cooked it."

They bounce through the door, shaking her trailer. The stove eyes quiver, the walls creak. "Ain't nothing to do round this place, Granmama," says Bloop. He hovers above her, sniffing at the spitting pot. Black face, white teeth, bullet head.

"Go pick you up some pecans," she says. "Say they bringing a good price now."

"Ain't picking up no pecans," he says and snorts. "Back ain't up to it."

He sits at the kitchen table, knuckling the scorch-ringed white Formica top, and Beanie sprawls on the couch, switching the TV on with the remote control, Louise's sole luxury.

"My back ain't gone be up to gathering no greens next time neither." Louise shakes cornmeal from a commissary cracker jar to a green bowl.

"Put some cracklins in that cornbread, Granmama," says Bloop. "Ain't had no cracklin cornbread in a month of Sundays."

"Not since middle of the week," she says. Though Bloop is no longer lovable, she finds it hard not to love him, not to be taken in by him—her first grand. "Quit that framming on that table fore I lose my mind."

He springs up and bebops into the living room and sprawls next to Beanie, long legs taking up half the mangy green carpet being daily reduced by junk. "Ain't nothing on that channel worth a damn," he says to Beanie.

"Look out I don't wash out yo mouth with soap powder!" Louise hollers. "Check on Little Angel for me. She napping on my bed."

Bloop snatches the remote from Beanie, who snatches it back. *The Price Is Right*. Money, money, money. Everybody laughing and shouting brand names and prices. That spinning wheel is what makes the world go round. Makes Louise sick. Bob Barker is a poor man's dream gone berserk. But he's like family.

"How long fore dinner, Granmama?" says Beanie.

"Bout thirty minutes," she says. She likes them there, though she never shows it, never says it, especially to Roper, who it seems she has spent the better part of her life trying to force to love his own flesh-and-blood boys. She had almost given up when she came into possession of the shoe. But what Louise likes best is not looking at the boys, just listening to them talk and pretending they are still chubby children with glossy curls like black grapes. Though lately she has quit pretending. She looks at them now, their great white shoes, Bloop's tomwalker legs. Nothing going on behind those eyes. Bodies outgrowing their minds—what little there is of their minds. Mostly, they just function from the senses: what to see next, what to taste next, what to feel, smell, touch next. Next not now. Now is never enough; same way with money. Louise figures if Roper doesn't take hold soon, the boys will become so jaded they'll need more and more jolts to their eyes, ears, noses, mouths, and unmentionables, to produce thrills.

"One of you boys go call the younguns in," she yells, "and tell yo daddy I got the cornbread on." She slides the iron skillet into the oven, heat rushing to her face. "Never mind bout Roper," she adds. The boys weren't going after him anyway, and she has to let Roper come to her. Of his own free will.

❖ ❖ ❖

By Monday morning, Louise figures she might have to extend her one-week deadline for Roper to come to her. Lying in her bed, she hears the Isuzu judder from Sweet's yard, up the dirt road to the highway. Yesterday, she'd been so sure he was coming around: all day moping about his trailer and yard, watching her from his recliner while she cleaned pike fish on the white table in her front yard. Ahab's boy, Little Ahab, had caught the slender, red-finned fish in the branch across the railroad tracks, where Louise used to fish with her daddy. Twice Louise almost broke down and went over to Roper's trailer with the paper-wrapped shoe in her apron pocket, but each time she rerouted her steps, pinching dead blooms from her mums and rearranging the junk in her yard. Not even a how do you do from either of them.

He knew.

How long since he has been to see the man? Lying in her bed, she tries to remember, afraid Roper will miss one of his scheduled visits and end up in jail again. And then realizes how laughable her worry about the probation officer is under the circumstances—Louise is on the verge of sicking the law on Roper for what might mean a murder charge. She will do it. She has to do it. For Little Taylor, for her grandboys, who she suspects would as soon commit murder as steal quarters from her change jar.

What drives Louise crazy, during the deadline week, is how she changes day to day; by turns feeling guilty about even considering turning Roper in, and then feeling justified. And when Friday rolls around and he hasn't come to her for the shoe, she begins to wonder who she will tell, when she tells, who will be more merciful toward her only son—Math Taylor or the law—and well understands what God went through when he sent his only son, Jesus, to the cross. A concept she doesn't come close to understanding, but believes in with all her heart to keep from winding up in hell. And finally she talks herself into feeling that to do otherwise, to not tell the truth, would be blasphemy. Forget for-the-good-of-the-grandboys, forget for-the-good-of-Roper-and-Math-Taylor. Louise's is a holy mission. Though she doesn't really fool herself; she is just keeping to what she's promised herself any way she can.

❖ ❖ ❖

She will go to Math Taylor, she decides. Four reasons: One, he is nearby; and two, she has reason to believe that he is a merciful man, a generous man (even during his lean years, following his regular visits to check up on Mama Lou, she would find a ten or twenty for Mama Lou and another ten or twenty for her church beneath plates and vases; and during his fat years, surprise one-hundred-dollar bills would spring alive and suspicious as Monopoly-game money—one for Mama Lou and another for her church). Three, she knows he respects her, even loves her, and might believe her if she tells him that Roper didn't kill his wife but evidently knows something about her disappearance. Number four and most important, Louise is betting on the influence and inspiration of Wainer Taylor's ghost. She has always relied on feelings, and she has a feeling that Little Taylor will know without knowing, will sense, that his daddy loved Louise, that Roper is Wainer Taylor's own son, making him Math Taylor's half brother, which nobody now knows except

Annie-the-Freedom-Rider, Louise, and Wainer Taylor's ghost.

"Law, gal, you something! Law, gal, you make me laugh." Wainer's smoke-roughened voice would tilt to the raw-board commissary ceiling with the tilt of his sun-bright face. He would rear in his chair behind the desk, where Louise stood with her time sheet and cotton-weighing tablet, and she would know the sadness behind those squinched aqua eyes (cotton business going to nothing, his wife sickly). Laughing with him, though knowing her place—a Negro woman—knowing when to stop laughing. But inching closer in her head and feeling him inch closer till at last they touched.

But that was after her husband Low got killed at the sawmill, two days after Low died, four days after Wainer Taylor had bought Louise a mess of mullet from the fish truck that stopped off at the commissary. She had gone straight home to fry the fish, hungry following a long, hot day in the cotton field. Scaling and frying the fish and before she could even sample anything save a salty fish tail, cleaning those same fish up off the floor. Grease and all. On her knees, Low standing over her, drunk, with his belt doubled. "Can't afford no fish from that white bastard."

"Ain't cost you nothing," she said, gazing up at his big brown face. "He give em to me."

"Yeah," Low said, striking her across the back with his belt, "but it costing you, ain't it?"

She sat on the greasy bare floor with her hands raised to ward off the next lick. "I ain't pay nothing," she said. The next lick blistered the lard-coated fingertips of her right hand, bent them backward.

"You think I don't know how come you ain't picking cotton with the rest of the niggers, huh?"

"I weighs up the cotton they pick," she said, scooting back on the slick boards, "you know that. I keep track of who pick how much and when."

"Cause you can write, huh? Old Pappy learn his girl youngun to write so she can lord it over us niggers other side of the track."

Same old reason for beating her; he always started out with something new, then linked it to her somehow acting superior. She scrambled up, tall and sturdy, with her planed face turned to him, but as far away from him as she could get with the wall at her back, unless she should sidle to the right and out the screen door. Which was what she had in mind.

"Ain't nobody make you marry me," she said—yelled. "Ain't nobody tell you to come after me cross them tracks."

He stepped closer, the overhead light shining on his gleaming black hair, his wrestler's body. He had a scar, like a wrinkle, on his forehead from a knife fight with another of the quarters' bullies. "Pappy got you b'lieving you better'n everbody else," he said, low and baiting. "Now old man Taylor doing the same thing." Another step forward, slipping, he balanced with his arms out, belt slicing the fish-smoky air.

Louise, with her long hands greasing the cool wall behind, stepped farther right. Almost to the door. She'd been through this before—lots of befores—and what generally worked best with Low was to keep him quarreling till he either passed out or she could give him the slip. Then spend the night at Pappy and Ida's pieced-together red house across the tracks. "Ain't nobody think they better'n nobody else," she said. "Ain't nobody mess with me neither. You just tanked up's all."

An alarm went off in her head—shouldn't have said that—and before she could lunge for the door, Low lunged for her and wrestled her to the floor, socking her in the face. Her left eye felt punched to the back of her head. She tried to scramble up, crawling toward the screen door, but he caught her by one ankle and yanked her back. Stuck to the wire screen were beetles like polished wood buttons, and beyond, people gathering, watching from her yard. They were used to Low and his ways. But this time he would have killed Louise if Wainer Taylor hadn't been sent for, if he hadn't stopped Low, because this time, for the first time in three years, Louise had fought back. Maybe because, groveling and scratching at the screen door, like a caged rat, she had seen, really seen, for the first time, the faces of the fieldhands, who looked up to her every day because she could write, now looking down on her because she was taking a whipping, and she was on her feet blowing and kicking and biting till the light overhead went out.

Two days later, when Wainer Taylor drove her home from the hospital, Old Ahab, foreman at the sawmill, was waiting with the news that Low was dead. While riding the carriage, his pants leg had got caught in the saw blade and he had been snatched into it. They said.

Then two nights later Wainer Taylor knocked on her door. When she opened it, he was standing there on the porch with the full moon at his back. Such a perfect circle, that moon.

"Tell me to go, gal," he said, "just say it and you know I will."

She didn't answer, only backed into the room and waited for him to step inside, waited for the moonlight runner to roll back on the floor as he closed the door. Breathing hard, smelling of willows and tobacco. Whiskey.

"You know how come I'm here, gal," he said. "You know I want you. I love you."

"You have Low kilt?"

"In a way I did. I won't lie."

"I ain't grieving," she said. "I ain't feel nothing."

"Been fish gigging," he said in high, proud monotone. "Got river sand in my boots."

"Take em off then."

He crossed the room to the chair before the window, sat, and began shucking off his boots, backlit by moonlight, that head, that cleft chin, those tilted-up eyes. Perfect as the moon.

"You have him kilt for me?"

"Law, gal, I'd do just about anything for you. But I did it for me too. I did it as a matter of pride, I did it cause I love you."

She waited, watching him, watching him rise from the chair and shed his shirt, his belt, his pants, his long slender body moon-bathed. That molded chest. Not a word, and the only sounds katydids outside the window and dogs barking way off. A train thundered, wailed, passed on the crossing south of the quarters, where Louise the girl had lived when Low had come calling . . . exactly when she couldn't remember. Not now. She watched Wainer walk toward the bed, testing each step, and when he got there, he caught her shoulders and began stroking her broken right arm, then, following her breath in the dark, kissed her. Tenderness, something new to Louise; feeling loved, something new to Louise. And she would come to know the difference between being in love and loving: being in love meant two people loving one another, not just one loving. Moonlight sucked him closer. In the dark of the bed, they were the same color.

"I reckon you thinking I could've called the law on Low," he said, lifting his lips from hers, "but we done that before; they don't do nothing."

"Hush!" she said. "Don't say nothing; we together now."

He kissed her again, then whispered. "Sometimes you have to whistle, gal, if you want the wind to blow."

❖ ❖ ❖

When Louise starts toward her old white station wagon, eyeing Roper sitting on his doorstep, she is not fully convinced that she will go to Math Taylor, but is hoping Roper will believe she is going. To make sure he knows what her mission is that cloudy, warm Saturday morning, she takes the shoe from her apron pocket, unwraps it, and holds it up.

His droopy eyes stretch and he stands, limping barefoot toward the car. Not the way it should have been, true, not the way she'd planned. When he gets to the front of the car, he holds out his right hand.

She shakes her head and sticks the shoe back into her pocket and drops the newspaper to the dirt with the fresh trash dragged up by the dogs during the night.

"What you up to, Mama?" he says.

"Up to making you own up to what you know bout

Lora Taylor," she says. "Up to making you stand for something."

"How's that?"

"I be on my way to take this shoe to Little Taylor, that what." She places one hand on top of her burry gray head. "Hear on the TV last night he been off on another trip looking at dead bodies."

"You think I kill that woman?"

"Nope. I think you didn't."

"I don't get it." He scratches his head.

"Gone make you face up to Little Taylor, make you tell what you know so the law know he ain't kill nobody. Gone make you prove to them boys in there you ain't kill nobody."

He laughs, props with both hands on the car hood, sounds like he's crying. "Ain't nobody gone believe I ain't done it, you know that."

"I don't know that."

"I messed up." He doesn't look at her, looks down at his long, thin feet in the damp dirt.

"What you did?"

"Find her dead that day. Find her passed-out dead on a road through that field I been mowing seem like since I was born."

She refuses to be taken in by his self-pity. "What kill her?"

"Don't know," he says, looking up now. "Don't look like nothing kill her, I mean, no blood on her body."

Turned to stone by what the answer might be to her next question, she asks anyway. "If she be laying in a road in that field, how come nobody ain't find her?"

"That where I mess up," he says, crying for real now,

low like a man choking. He turns his back to her; his boy-
ish shoulders shake. "I get scared somebody think I do
it—I mean, and me on probation and all—so I take up
her body and chunk it in that old well cross the field."

Louise waits, hand on the shoe, trying to picture him
doing that, but can't.

"Chunk bricks in on top of the body's what I do." He
turns around, facing Louise square. "I ain't kill that lady,
you know that. But gone look like I do it if that shoe turn
up now."

"You find the shoe later?" says Louise. "Where it fall
off, right?"

"Yessum," he says, "and then a tornado come and blow
a tree down on the well . . ." He pauses, maybe waiting
for her reaction to news of a tornado, then adds, "And
then them boys get hold of that shoe and go to blackmailing me."

"I know the rest of it, you do too," she says, refusing to
be taken in by her own fear of tornadoes. "Them boys
belief you kill her, don't see nothing wrong in that;
killing ain't no more to them than stealing quarters out
of my change jar."

"I ain't their mama," he says, drying up, puffing up.
"What I know bout raising no younguns?"

"You bout to mess up worser now," she says and
snatches at the stuck car door. "You bout to get on my
badside for sho."

"So what you wanting me to do is turn myself in and
prove something they ain't no way a-proving?"

She just stands there, knowing he is right, but knowing
she is right too.

"Give me the shoe, Mama." He holds out his hand,

starts around the car. "Ain't no way without that shoe anybody gone blame me. That lady ain't gone come back to life just cause I tell. Get it?"

"Then how you gone make them boys know you ain't kill her, how you gone shut them up?"

"I done shut em up."

"How's that?"

"Find drugs on em."

She has to latch both hands on the car door to keep from falling. "Just what I mean," she says. "Somebody gotta stand for something, somebody gotta take a hold."

"Why me, Mama?"

"Ain't nobody else."

10

Louise doesn't give the shoe to Roper, but agrees he can't prove what he can't prove—that he didn't kill Lora Taylor—and Lora Taylor will be no less dead if her body is found. She tries to shame him though, for Jesus's sake, into telling Little Taylor and letting him get on with his life—she isn't sure how practical that is either—then gets on with her own modified plans to make Roper stand for something, to make him set an example for the boys and take charge of the quarters. She would have liked for Roper to come to her of his own accord, but as Wainer Taylor used to say, sometimes you have to whistle if you want the wind to blow. What she demands of Roper is almost as hard as proving he had nothing to do with the death of Math Taylor's wife, much like Jesus dying on the cross for our sins: Roper has to clean up the quarters, for starters, beginning with the junk he has hauled from the dumpsters to Louise's yard, making the boys work with him, and he has to work regular hours for Taylor—she shakes the shoe at him—and pay for the food she cooks. He has to dip all the dogs in burnt motor oil and sulfur to get rid of the mange; he has to make the boys do their homework, make them go to school during the day and stay home at night, and in the evenings, after school, make them pick up pecans and collect aluminum cans from the dumpsters to sell. Lastly, Roper has to get all the children in the quarters to church for the Christmas play, hopefully luring the adults in, where the preacher will dose them with the gospel, and Louise will slam them with civic duty. If Roper doesn't do all this by Christmas, she will snitch on him, she will take the shoe to Math Taylor. She has nothing to lose, she is dying, she says. Roper tucks his chin, checks her nickel-plated eyes for trickery, and knows she is telling the truth, but when he asks when she will die and of what, she lies about the time and tells him somewhere around Christmas, though she expects she'll live till next season, and doesn't mention she is dying of the same old ailment as everybody else since Adam.

As he heads for his trailer, she calls out, "If you thinking bout waiting till I be dead and gone to get this shoe, don't. I plan on making good on my threat before I go. I plan on making you stand for something, something good."

"I ain't think that, Mama, I just gotta get off by myself and study."

"No more studying. Clean my yard up. Now. Get that truck and start chunking junk on it."

"Yessum." He sidesteps through the ragged hedge, gets into the Isuzu, starts it, and backs out to the road. He pulls into Louise's yard, wedging between her old white station wagon and the junk heap.

"Now go get them lazy boys from in front of that TV in yonder." She sits on a chair by the doorsteps while he goes inside for the boys, and doesn't even try to eavesdrop when he shuts the door. Half the time she can't make out what the boys are saying anyway, but now she can tell by loud puffing and guffawing and sudden whispers that they are being threatened, shamed, maybe blackmailed. After ten minutes, Roper lopes down the doorsteps with the boys following, dressed up, sullen, seething. Roper pitches a five-gallon can to the back of the truck and Beanie matches him by pitching some balled-up rags. Then Bloop tosses a red plastic cup, then Roper an oil can, like a hand grenade, and so on. As if one is afraid of outworking the other. Roper eyes Louise, perched on the chair, sunning with her arms crossed. Almost regal in her purple turban and purple shirt and skirt, almost black as the window above her head.

When she looks down she likes to see something new, something young covering her old skin, to remind her of her young years when she was beautiful and her body was at ease, because, for a fact, living old is like not living at all, because for a fact a young outfit takes her back to the time when Wainer Taylor had bought her a new white flared dress to wear to the Swanoochee County court-house to register to vote. Between them, that fair October day, with the sun glaring on the concrete side-walk, the understanding that he was saying to the white world that he was proud of this black woman by his side—*Law, gal, you something. Law, gal, you make me laugh.* No words at the moment, though, just the two of them pacing up the concrete walk to the red brick courthouse, not even touching, him tall and stringy tough with his bright face lifted; and her, just as tall, but sturdy built, chiseled mahogany. "Law, gal, you a sight in that dress," he whispered. "I tell the world that, I tell the world I love you." But of course, he never did, not in words, and of course she didn't expect it. Theirs was a world of defined lines they toed up to but never stepped across in public.

❖ ❖ ❖

Less than a year after Low died, Louise gave birth to her second baby—her first baby had been stillborn—this time a boy: colicky, runty like Louise's daddy, with cream-brown skin the only clue that Roper's father might be Wainer Taylor, that next breast to Roper, one-year-old Math might be Roper's half brother. Not that Louise and Wainer were listening for what people were saying. Following Wainer's wife Hallie's death, just one month after Roper was born, they were at first spelled by guilt and the sudden easy accessibility to one another inside the big green house across from the commissary.

Every evening, Louise would wait till Wainer got home from the turpentine woods or commissary, then hike out with her baby toward the cabin in the quarters. But just as she and Wainer had drifted apart, they soon drifted back together, watching their babies grow and play in the roomy old house and oak-shady yard. Wainer playing with them both, bringing them candy from the commissary, letting them ride his back, showing no favoritism for the chubby blond child. An odd happy family during the daylight hours. But Louise always returned to her shack in the quarters at night.

"Gal, you don't have to go," Wainer would say. And she'd say, "Yeah, I do," and he wouldn't argue that point because there was really no point to argue and no point in arguing.

She had her baby and he had his.

He would take Math riding in his pickup, leaving Roper clawing at the latched screen door and crying, "Go, go, go." When Wainer tried to take him, Louise would claim it was Roper's nap time or he was coming down with something. Then one hot summer day Wainer stopped his pickup under the oaks out front, sailed out with his face red, stomped up the doorsteps and across the wide moldy-green porch, and yanked at the screen door till Louise unlatched it. He reached down, scooped up Roper, and glared at her. "Don't you cross me on this, woman," he said and stomped back to the truck and stood Roper in the seat between him and Math. One white-headed with flossy ringlets, the other black-headed with squiggly curls, like sheep's wool.

The next morning Louise didn't show up at the big house. Come evening, Wainer was standing inside her kitchen, where she was putting up tomatoes, her crawling baby pulling up on Wainer's boot tops. He picked up Roper, jiggling him in his long-muscled arms.

"Law, gal," he said, "don't do this to me. I know what you trying to say and from now on I'll do what you say do. It's just . . ."

"You ain't no fool, Wainer Taylor," she said with her hands on her hips and tomato juice staining her white apron.

His squinched aqua eyes turned teary. "I am when it comes to you and my boys," he said, taking back the yellow pencil Roper had slipped from his shirt pocket to gnaw on.

"Well," she said, "you bout to mess em up big time. Bout to mess us up too, cause they's lines I cross and lines I don't cross. Less you ready to pick up and move off Upnorth." She'd heard somewhere that Negroes and whites mixed in that place called Upnorth.

Wainer passed Roper to her. "It's a sorry world, ain't it, gal?"

"It be the chirren what suffer cause of fools like you."

He just stood there.

"Now go on," she said. "Git! I be over soon as I get this tomato juice off my hands."

He left, driving, and she followed, walking.

❖ ❖ ❖

After the large pieces of junk are loaded, Roper gets into the Isuzu and the boys start around the other side. "Going to the dumpster," Roper calls to Louise.

"I give you fifteen minutes," she says and pats the shoe in her pocket. She gazes up at the sun peeping through scalloped white clouds above the quarters.

"Fifteen minutes! Granmama!" Bloop takes off his turned-around cap and swats at the hood of the battered blue Isuzu.

"Try and make it in ten," she says, getting up and going inside, "and rake up the rest of that paper and plastic when you get back." And then to God she says low, "Lord in heaven, forgive me. Big Taylor, forgive me. Ain't but a couple more weeks misery for Little Taylor, but be a whole lifetime for my people."

In what she estimates to be about twenty minutes they are back—she doesn't expect perfection, not yet—quarreling and sweating and grumbling about being tired. The boys are. Roper just keeps bouncing about with the rake, making tiny piles of trash for the boys to pick up; they gather handfuls of mixed dirt, grass, paper, and plastic, holding it away from their khaki shorts and white T-shirts. Those fine clothes Louise bought with her babysitting money to keep them from maybe robbing somebody to stay in style.

Louise, watching from the doorway, steps gingerly down the steps and sits in the chair again, staring at the clean rake marks over combed yellow grass, oddly sprouting after so long under cover of a plywood square.

Dogs ramble and rest in the shade of the chinaberry tree, scratching their molting hides. Men wander past, on their way to Sweet's house, and call out to Roper and the boys, "Mama put y'all to work, huh?" Roper mumbles, raking. The boys mumble, gathering trash. Children sidle around the hedge, grinning, and eye the cleanup detail. Little Angel peeps from behind Louise's trailer and stands sucking her thumb, then like an ant drawn to sugar, creeps over and crawls onto Louise's lap.

"Where yo mama, baby?" says Louise, bouncing her knees. "She know where you be?"

Little Angel shrugs and snuggles into Louise's drooped bosom.

Louise laughs and spanks Little Angel's leg. "She know where to look if she want you. Right, baby?"

Little Angel gazes up with hot, fluid eyes. "Mama getting her another baby. Say I ain't gone be her baby no more."

"Well, you be my baby." Louise kisses her on her dry brown forehead. Then mumbles to herself, "Uh uh! Like that woman need another baby! After another check, what it is."

Little Angel shifts to watch as Roper rakes lazily toward the chinaberry tree, shooing the dogs from their wallowed-out spots in the damp, gray dirt.

Preacher's long white car motors around the curve in front of Sweet's house, the waxed roof spiking light as it passes from shade to sun stripes.

"See where he stop at," Louise says to Little Angel, "see who he visit."

Preacher steers the car carefully through the hedge gap and parks behind Louise's station wagon—one car dull, the other bright, but both white, just cars. He gets out and strolls toward the blue trailer. Bald head gleaming like his car. Bronze and erect as a statue. White shirt, black suit, black shoes. His crinkled hazel eyes are fixed on Roper and the boys, who look suddenly industrious and pious, yet otherwise unfazed by the holy presence on unholy ground.

Louise tries to mask her pride: usually she can count on one of Preacher's visits when the children have wrecked her house, or a fight between the boys is in full swing. Or a bitch dog is giving birth under Louise's very doorsteps.

She holds her head high. "How you today, Preacher?" she says.

"Awright, Sister Louise. How you faring?" He sits on the doorsteps with one smart black shoe planted on a mosaic of crushed red glass. Hikes the legs of his black gabardine pants to relieve his blunt jacked knees. "Look like you got these boys working," he says loud, as if for their benefit.

Roper rakes around the other side of the station wagon; the boys and Roper's red cur follow the trail of rake tines.

"Out visiting," Preacher says and interlocks his long bronze fingers in the V of his spread legs.

Little Angel, dozing, has slid down on Louise's lap, so that her bare heels dangle at Louise's shins. Louise lifts the child higher, cuddles her to her bosom. Rocking. "Well, you know I always be glad of a visit," she says. Lie.

"But they folk herebouts what need a visit much as me." Truth.

Preacher rares back, propping his elbows on the next-highest step.

Roper's red cur bitch ambles from behind the station wagon toward the road. A primer-gray car passes with the trunk lid propped up with a stick. Four children sit inside the trunk with eight brown legs hooked over the bumper. The dog stares at the car, then listing left, keeps walking.

"You want these folk to show up for one of yo fine sermons, Preacher, you gotta go get em," says Louise. "You gotta bump em up."

"Yes ma'am," he says. "That the Lord's truth. Look like Saturday just always catch me right for visiting."

Louise thinks, but doesn't say, never says, If you wouldn't spend half your time waxing that car, you could get here during the week before everybody gets to drinking and carousing. Someday she'll say it. But not today. Why does she always have to tell everybody what to do, where to do it, how to do it. and when to do it?

"Looking good out here," Preacher says loud, but Roper and the boys remain hidden behind the station wagon with just the tops of their heads showing. Digging to China with that rake. "That a pretty girlbaby, ain't she?" says Preacher, turning his full attention on somebody who can't dodge him, somebody sleeping.

Louise gazes down at Little Angel, warmed by sunshine on one side and Louise's body heat on the other. "Her mama be right over there," she says, nodding toward the house behind her trailer. "Might take this baby here to church if you ask her right. Might let her be in the Christmas play if you build it up to be something."

She wags her head. "Ain't no Christmas play without no angel, and ain't no point in all that big money Little Taylor give us if ain't no young peoples to spend it on."

No answer, and Louise knows he has a coward heart, and feels for him: he has been run off from every house in the quarters since he came to this church a couple of years ago. But she suspects that Preacher would like to keep his church neat and solemn, and programs for the young people would wreck his sacred routine.

"Next week, I see if I can't make it over there on Friday," he says and stands, and the heads showing over the station-wagon roof duck low.

"Make it Thursday," says Louise. "Give folk a little time before they gear up for the weekend."

"Yes ma'am," he says, strolling off toward his waxed white car with his hands in his fine pants pockets. "See you at church tomorrow, Sister Louise."

"I be there." She buries her nose in the sweet-sunned braids of Little Angel's bound head. "Man ain't nothing but a coward," she says low, "ain't never gone get nobody to church talking down to them like that."

Soon, the boys begin complaining of hunger and thirst, and Roper starts toward the gap in the hedge, to go to the juke and get them a cold drink. Louise calls him back. "Drink you some water out of that spigot." She nods toward the spigot bracketed to the blue wall of her trailer.

By sundown, the yard is clean, following two more trips to the dumpster, and still Louise watches from her chair by the doorsteps, filing cleaning plans in her mind for the rest of the quarters, where Saturday-night racket is loading the air—music, laughter, lone shouts that signify people on the move.

11

That night Louise lies in her bed and waits for sleep, total silence and darkness since she has quit dreaming, or if she dreams she can never remember dreaming, and fears she's thwarted her dreams by always seeking out silence and darkness. Though she believes the New Testament promise of the Rapture in the twinkling of an eye, the Lord's Second Coming, she does hope that her dark, quiet sleep of death, her soon-to-be home in the grave, will last long enough for her to enjoy the peace. That she will be aware of that peace.

She listens to the boys in their bedroom, beyond the thin paneled wall by her bed, knocking about and quarreling above the wild music of the radio. Usually she tries to stay awake long enough to make sure they don't slip out, but this time Roper has threatened them and they've retired to their room, and he has gone on to his trailer, or out wandering the quarters. In the next room, the floor knocks, the walls knock, and Louise laments the usual peace of her trailer during their usual night outings. No more. She arranges the hard shoe under her pillow so that it feels like a lump in the feathers. She will sleep in her grave.

When finally her dark sleep overtakes her, a sweet tingling from her face down to the hardened joints of her knees and feet, she is awakened suddenly by a slice of light through her bedroom door and the silhouette of Bloop's leggy body standing by her bed, bending and sorting through her clothes on the floor. She waits, watching him get down on his knees and feel beneath her bed. He stands up, gazes down at her, then creeps out, easing the door shut behind him.

She sits up, listening to him tiptoeing toward the living room, whispering out the front door to somebody. Roper. Low fussing. Can't find the shoe. Not in the kitchen, not under the couch where she always sits, not in her apron pocket on the floor in her bedroom.

❖ ❖ ❖

Sunday morning, Louise's imposed day of rest, she carries the shoe in her great black pocketbook to church, knowing the boys are roaming where they will, or maybe ransacking her trailer with Roper's help. Good, give them something to do. Keep them busy and out of trouble. She won't work them today, but tomorrow she has plans.

On second thought, maybe she will work them today—ox is in the ditch, so to speak. She raises her right hand, "Excuse me, Preacher."

He looks at her, has been looking at her, stops droning on about the Prodigal Son, and says, "What, Sister Louise?"

"I be thinking," she says, "since we both done know that one by heart, and ain't nobody else here today, maybe we just save it till next Sunday when Sister Mary Beth be back."

❖ ❖ ❖

Generally ailing on the first school day of the week, the boys catch the bus at the highway Monday morning, Roper seeing them off, then heading for the Taylor place to work. All of this Louise hears from her clean front yard with rake marks on the dirt and combed grass. Throughout the sunny warm day, she keeps going to her front door to look at the rake marks and watch the children play and the sparrows flurry in the chinaberry tree, how they drop like the leaves and flock to her collard patch.

In the pecan tree that grows on Sweet's side of the hedge but branches out over Louise's side, crows big as chickens caw and ricochet from the naked branches to the dirt, snitching pecans. She listens out, around the sore-throated cawing of crows, but hears only a bad imitation of turkey calls—Ahab with his condom turkey caller.

Louise misses the blackbirds. Of all the ordinary, grounding things she misses from her past—the good old days—she misses most the blackbirds. She misses their capering in the gray fall skies—hundreds and hundreds—visiting farm to farm with chirpy babbling, gleaning corn left in the fields by the pickers. Whole flocks of blackbirds would swoop unbroken to the oaks in Withers and bat the acorns from the branches to the tin roofs.

Inside the electric-lit trailer, she opens her windows, but the light from outside isn't light enough to suit her. The black paint of the jalousies hoods the brightness, the bluish fall light. She starts scraping paint from her front windows.

When the boys get in from school, famished, fussing, and crashed in front of the TV, she doesn't say a word, just keeps scraping till Roper gets in, then gives them their orders for the evening. Starting with the road and road shoulders along the curve of the quarters, they will pick up trash and pack it into croaker sacks.

"Hell, man," Beanie says to Roper, who hands him a sack, "that ain't even our trash."

Louise answers by including the yards of the rest of the quarters.

"Granmama," whines Bloop, "it just about nighttime."

Standing in the doorway, she gazes west at the sun wallowing behind the pines. "You got a good hour of daylight," she says.

Roper sets out with his sack slung over his left shoulder, the boys following up the sandy road, with sacks dragging over their footprints. Dogs and people watch the miracle from the dusky yards and roadsides.

While Roper and the boys work, Louise scrapes, kitchen window and living-room windows, smudgy bright even filling with dusk. When the women, whose children Louise keeps, stop by to pick up their children, Louise keeps scraping paint. If she stops now she might stop forever; if she takes a good, hard, close-up look at her sorry neighbors, she might repaint the windows she's scraped.

Take Sweet, for instance, whose falling-down, filthy house Louise stands facing through a peephole of black paint. Half porch with a room on the west end, a sun-rotted red curtain on the window over the porch. Sweet's law office, as she calls it, where she grants divorces and draws up agreements between the newly divorced parties: who gets the kids, who gets the car, who gets the furniture. All free, though anybody who has had any dealings with her will tell you she expects favors in return.

Louise can only guess what the favors might be.

She starts on the window in her bedroom, and works her way to the north window in the boys' room. Watching Roper and the boys straggling with their sacks along the north curve of the road, picking up paper and bottles and cans—lazy-looking, sullen, sassing at their jeering neighbors.

❖ ❖ ❖

The next evening, while Roper and the boys work, Louise begins scraping paint again, this time the east windows overlooking the other shacks hiding Roper and the boys, who she catches glimpses of now and then between the patched houses and trailers and droopy lines of clothes, between the peeling white sycamore trunks and mossy oaks.

Somebody has been stealing clothes off clotheslines; somebody even stole a cast-iron washpot from Lucy and it ended up in the yard of Ahab's juke—a big fight. Ahab claimed he bought it from Somebody, but wouldn't say who. Louise is afraid one of the boys, or both, is stealing and selling stolen goods, as they say on the TV news.

Scraping the tiny window of the bathroom, she spies Roper and Beanie picking paper, like cotton, from a section of wire fence in front of the juke, then Bloop stalking off, slinging his sack, and Roper chasing him down, tackling him, yanking him up by the scruff of his neck. A group of men from the juke stand, laughing, watching. Then Roper with his hands on his hips talking to them, mad looks, then Walleyed Willie and Boss picking paper from the fence like berries from briers.

Dusk filling with dark, Louise, scraping the east windows of the living room, watches the boys dragging full sacks toward the south curve and Roper wandering toward the juke. She doesn't expect miracles, not yet.

❖ ❖ ❖

Later, when Roper comes walking through the yard in the light-streaked dark, Louise is waiting in the chair by her doorsteps in a rectangle of light from the front living-room windows. He glances toward her lit trailer and spies her sitting on the chair. Stops and stands there rocking on his toes. The TV inside sounds louder.

"They ain't started on no lessons in there yet," she says, shaking the shoe at him.

"What the . . . ?"

"You got to bump em up," she says, "get em going."

"I ain't no teacher." He walks toward her, stops a few yards away.

"But you their daddy. Go make like one for a change."

He snorts, walks past her up the doorsteps. Steps into the living room and switches off the TV. Yelps and feet slapping the floor. "Man, we was watching that!"

"Gotta do your lessons, she says." Roper closes the front door.

Much quarreling, then a light in the kitchen shows through the small square window on the dirt outside. Chairs scrape back from the table.

"I ain't got no homework." Beanie.

"I do mine at school." Bloop.

"Read the books. Don't matter if you done read the whole thing, read the books." Roper.

A book slaps the table. Quiet except for blowing and snorting. Ten minutes and the TV clicks on, laughter and jabbering. Then Roper comes walking out the door, down the doorsteps.

"They got their lessons," he says to Louise and angles toward his trailer, head down.

"I wadn't borned yesterday," she says. "Ten minutes ain't enough time for them boys and them a-failing in their grades."

"I get em twenty tomorrow night."

"And tonight," she says, "you better not be keeping them up to search for no shoe."

He looks back, walking. "Ain't no peace to be had," he says.

"That the Lord's truth."

❖ ❖ ❖

From the south window of the kitchen, Louise oversees Roper's work detail along the curve in front of the church. She watches through growing gashes in the black paint: a broken dirt dauber's adobe burrow in the upper left corner of the metal window, with each of its four cells containing living worms for the dauber's young to feed on when they hatch; and beyond the window, smoke from the trash fires unraveling from tangles of flames; lazy fires and slow smoke and boys and girls policing the road, at times scattering more trash than they collect in their croaker sacks, but doubling back when Roper yells at them. Dogs straggle behind, resting on their haunches to scratch. Now and then a cola can sails from hand to hand, over heads, then somebody has to go after it. A ragtag work detail, to be sure, and Louise marvels, in spite of her threats, that Roper has stuck with the project, that he has enlisted so much help. She suspects he is blackmailing half the quarters and thinks of his tactics as shameful till she recognizes the same tactics used by herself.

Along the broomsage stretch, between the church cemetery and the highway, Sweet ambles with her hands on her back pushing out her stomach, stooping stiffly to pick up a brickbat or a scrap of paper when the mood strikes her. First time Louise has ever seen that tramp work!

Has to be blackmail.

Day after day, gray clouds gather as if the smoke of trash fires has clogged the sky—burning tires, cardboard boxes, tree limbs, and leaves. The swagged blue Isuzu idles along the road, loaded with tire rims and iron bedsteads and even the solitary, pointless section of wire fence from the foreground of the juke, the same wire section that has been stomped down, walked around and lately even worked on. All is gray, except for the billowing blond broomsage that appears torched by sunlight. Bright as the inside of Louise's trailer since she has scraped most of her windows—one to go in the kitchen.

Scraping the last window, she watches for the work crew to show along the road in front of her trailer, and listens to the coming ruckus of kids and dogs and grownups—still fussing but laughing more than before.

Last window done, she watches Roper stick a match to the last leaf pile along the road, while the kids and grownups toss paper and limbs to the pyre, a real bonfire. Children romp round it. Flies swarm and dogs moil. A song somewhere.

Louise parades end to end of her trailer, eyeing through the scraped and polished windows the circle of fires burning low along the loop, all the way to the front again and the final fire.

She marches out the door with an armload of magazines from the boys' room and steps among the dogs and children and grownups and drops the magazines onto the fire. *Penthouse* cover girl blazing, breasts up in the fire.

12

Dogs' yelps and children's yells arch over the quarters, where the fires smolder under the same hood of clouds from yesterday.

Roper stands beneath the chinaberry tree, leafless but pronged with withering berry spikes. Before a fifty-five-gallon drum of burnt motor oil and sulfur, he waits for the first dog to skid in behind the first boy, then reaches down and lifts the mangy white dog with its hairless tucked tail and drops it into the drum. The dog scamps, oily black, over the lip of the drum and scuttles off, scrubbing on the rake-marked dirt.

Dogs coming from all the yards of the quarters on the ends of ropes—choking, dodging, but ending up in the drum, with Roper as oily black and sulfur smelly as any of them.

Louise, in her chair by the door, fans houseflies and watches the children and dogs, watches Roper, who seems to be enjoying their torture. A mangy fice wags around her knees and she kicks at him.

"Git on away from here, sir!" she says. He leaps back and shakes, speckling her orange skirt and shirt with oil.

Beanie, coming out of the trailer, steps aside, laughing. "Phew, Granmama, you smell like rotten eggs."

She stands, scrubbing the tail of her skirt and fussing.

"You the one after us to dip dogs," he says to her, and

then to Roper, "Ain't that right, old man?"

"That right," says Roper and lifts another dog over the drum and drops it like a rock.

Old man. As close to *Daddy* as Louise has come to hearing from either of the boys. She likes that. Though she suspects the old man has taken the young men to steal axle grease from that sidetracked boxcar near the railroad overpass. Bloop, next to the drum, waits for the dogs to clamber over the top, grabs them and smears their raw spots with a rag dipped in axle grease. Like Roper, Bloop in his ruined uniform of white T-shirt and khaki shorts looks too mischievously eager, which to Louise's way of thinking means he considers himself to be one up on her.

Again she sits, watching the children tugging their dogs on ropes, and now and then calls one over to sit on her lap.

"Look just like a angel," she says to Tiffany, six years old with hornlike braids. "You make a pretty angel for the church Christmas play."

The little girl squirms, hops to the dirt. "I be a angel, say Miss Louise," she tells the other children.

"You tell yo mama," says Louise, swatting a fly on her arm. "Tell Lorena I say she let you run harum-scarum all over the place, she can let you come to church."

Another little girl, with an old face and a scrawny body, steps up to Louise's chair and starts flapping her arms like wings. "Miss Louise, I be the best angel." Her filthy blue shift rides up and down, showing crusty stick legs.

"Lord need all the angels he can get," Louise says and laughs sadly. Pinworms.

Another girl steps up and poses for Miss Louise, then

another, and then all the little boys released from their
dog ropes, till Louise has her own Christmas play going
in her own front yard. One of the older boys is Joseph,
and a ten-year-old girl with sprouting breasts is Mary. She
looks as if she is truly pregnant, pooched stomach, veiny
feet. And though Louise keeps telling the children the
Christmas story and playing with them, she becomes sad
and wonders if the church play is worth the effort. If getting Roper to blackmail half the quarters—that's how it
will end up, she expects—can work a miracle, which is
what it will take to make them stand for something. Yes,
her plan has expanded to making the entire quarters
stand for something, something good.

"I be tired now," she says to the children, and gets up
and hobbles inside, where the smell of baking sweet
potatoes permeates the bright trailer. She closes her
eyes, walking.

She's not God.

But when she hears a car drive up to the yard, and
steps to the door to see Roper's probation officer sitting
inside while Roper talks to him through the window, she
is heartened to see Roper waving his hand about the
quarters. Finally, he isn't using going to see the man as
an excuse not to go to work; he is using work as an
excuse not to go to see the man.

❖ ❖ ❖

Roper and the boys watch TV that night, while Louise
watches them: Beanie on his stomach on the floor with
his stained heels high, and Bloop taking up half of
Louise's couch space with his head almost in her lap,
sledlike feet hung off the other end. Roper is perched on

the chair by the door as if he is on the verge of leaving.

Eleven-o'clock news and no mention of Lora Taylor so far. Roper yawns, stretches, stands, during the commercials.

Louise is working on the old Santa suit from the church, whipstitching the yellowing fur cuff on the right leg, where it was almost ripped off last year. By Louise. Yes, she has played Santa—sometimes to a near-empty church—but no more. No more empty church at Christmas and no more playing Santa for Louise. She may even step down from her position as church secretary—let these young people take hold—but knows she'll have to remain as treasurer, guarding the money she's hoarded and banked and protected through more preachers than she can remember.

"What that for?" says Roper, pointing at the Santa suit.

"You," she says. "You gone play Santy Claus at the church, come Christmas."

Bloop bobs his head, laughing; Beanie laughs. The people on the TV laugh—a preview of some old woman doctor talking dirty on the David Letterman Show. Little children and old people talking sex on TV are always good for a laugh.

"Me?" says Roper. "I ain't wearing no Santy Claus outfit."

Louise shakes out the pants, starts stitching the other fur cuff.

Roper heads for the door. "Go get you another fool."

"Update on the Lora Taylor case," says the smiley anchorwoman on the TV news, and drops her smile as she fills in the audience on the case background with a couple of sentences. "Still, false leads continue to filter in, but the missing woman remains missing and the Taylor family waits." Previously filmed shots of Math Taylor and the Taylor place flash across the screen, stagnant as the news.

❖ ❖ ❖

For the most part, what Louise remembers about Lora Taylor are sketchy episodes, gradating images, flashbacks of a person now dead from the perspective of one still living, one who feels a bit guilty for not remembering better and more: A young woman, cute but not pretty, petite, with long blond hair and green-gray eyes, sliding out of Little Taylor's pickup behind him and shrinking from the mangy, tail-switching dogs. Gold jewelry, shorts, strong tanned legs and pink toenails peeping from brown sandals. The sun was shining that morning.

"Mama Lou," said Little Taylor, grinning, "this is Lora, my new wife. She can cook, too."

A ribby black dog licked Lora's hand and she jerked back, leaning close to Little Taylor, who was leaning on the truck.

"Git on away from here, dogs!" Louise on the doorsteps clapped her hands. "Y'all come on in."

"Ain't got but a minute," said Little Taylor. The girl squinted at Louise and squirmed. She twined one slim golden arm around Little Taylor's arm and laced her ringed fingers into his.

Louise thought maybe she was shy, hoped she was shy, hoped she was more humble than she looked. Was glad she could cook.

If Louise saw Lora Taylor again before the child was born, she couldn't remember—she tried but couldn't remember—could remember only Little Taylor's tall slim body going to fat and the even features of his boy face pushing down and out over the weeks and months and years he stopped by, rushing to and from jobs to check on Mama Lou and eat her biscuit pudding and drop ten- and twenty-dollar bills in secret places.

He had told Louise about the baby girl with blond curls long before Louise saw her—a standing baby in the front seat next to her mother in a green car.

Lora Taylor, now not shy; there was no mistaking that she wasn't shy, she wasn't humble but haughty, with her blond hair sleek in a ponytail and her face made-up like a Sears mannequin's. Black eyeliner that made her green-gray eyes look small and hard. No smile.

She didn't get out of the green car. She sat with her diamond-ringed fingers on the black steering wheel and talked to Louise through the half-open window.

"I'm looking for some household help," she said. "Somebody to iron especially." Louise walked to the car to get a better look at the little girl with blond ringlets and Wainer Taylor's squinched aqua eyes. The child crawled across her mama's lap and hung to the window and smiled. Louise couldn't resist touching one of the blond ringlets circling her rosy round face.

"Ooo, what a pretty girlbaby," said Louise. "Look just like her granddaddy."

Lora Taylor lifted the child from her lap with rough hands and tried to set her on the seat beside her. The child's chubby knees locked and she toddled to the other side of the seat and spread her dimpled hands on the green-tinted glass.

The green car's engine still purred. Air-conditioner on

high and vents batting smells of leather, cigarettes, and perfume.

Louise never ironed Lora Taylor's clothes and couldn't remember why—whether she had said no she was too busy or had said yes and the clothes never came. Louise would have said yes, she believes now, just to get to see again that baby who looked so much like Wainer Taylor.

What Louise remembers best is the flash of two decades—the seventies and the eighties—and Little Taylor high-flying in a string of new pickups, then going into bankruptcy and losing the Taylor land, and somehow mysterious to Louise, pulling up by his bootstraps, as Wainer would have said, and starting over, low-flying and scaling down, whipped-looking but not whipped.

Throughout those decades, Louise remembers, or thinks she remembers, seeing that unchanged haughty face belonging to Lora Taylor behind the green-tinted windows of the green car in passing, but she doubts it because Lora Taylor wouldn't have been driving around the quarters—wouldn't have been driving the same car, an old car—and Louise wouldn't have seen her anywhere else. But she heard and heard, and saw on Little Taylor's changing face, that the Taylor household was in need of more than just its clothes ironed.

13

Next day it rains, starting with a warm drizzle and building to a steady, cold downpour that pounds like acorns on the roof and walls of Louise's stuffy, gaseous trailer. So much racket it overpowers the squeals and shouts of the children and the TV. Almost pickup time—not that the mothers are ever on time—and the children are as weary of Louise as she is of them.

After six and abnormally dark and still Lucy's two children are plundering and spilling and fussing. Little Angel is nestled on the couch under a scrapwork quilt, sucking her thumb and plucking at her braids, drowsy eyes fastened on Louise in the kitchen, stirring the pot of vegetable soup she has concocted out of hambone and leftovers.

"Look like ain't nobody but me got a clock," Louise mumbles, then remembers that one of the children just broke her old hand-wound alarm clock, and yells at Tony, wrapping his sister in toilet paper. "Stop that, mister. Y'all roll up ever bit of that paper and put it back, you hear?"

The tiny boy with bushy hair begins stripping the paper from his sister's body, and when the front door swings wide and Lucy appears in her white nurse's uniform, both children dash out the door into the rain with toilet paper flying like kite tails.

"Miss Louise," says Lucy, peeping around the doorway,

"Dreamer say for me to pick up Angel cause she be late."

Little Angel sits up, then stands, dragging the quilt from the couch to the door.

"Leave the quilt, baby," calls Louise, chipping cabbage into the boiling soup.

Little Angel drops the quilt and follows the others out into the rain, leaving the door open.

When Louise gets done, she goes over, picks up the quilt, and starts to close the door. She sees Lucy's old white Cadillac still parked in front of Louise's trailer, with white smoke billowing from the tailpipe. Toilet tissue sogging into the dirt from the trailer door to the car, and the three children hopping from front to back seats. Lucy is standing on Sweet's porch, talking to her.

Carrying the body-warmed quilt to the couch, Louise folds it. "If I know that woman gone run her mouth all day, I let that baby take this quilt to wrop up in. That old lottery—all that woman study."

Louise turns off the TV, then starts picking up picture-puzzle pieces, now so scattered nobody could ever put together Mickey Mouse again, then picks up the clock, forever stopped on six. Listening to the drumroll of rain on tin, she goes to the kitchen and drops the puzzle and the broken clock into the cuffed paper sack that holds her garbage. She takes a bowl from the stack in the cabinet above her kitchen-table window, glancing out at the white rain, the white car, the white smoke from the tailpipe, and Lucy on Sweet's porch. She considers going out and bringing the children back inside and feeding them some of her vegetable soup. Feels guilty as she sits down and starts eating, but can't help enjoying the hot tomatoey soup. Even watching the white car through the window, still and dark inside now, then big-butted Lucy in her white nurse's uniform trotting back across the yard to the car.

"Bout time," says Louise, spooning a hunk of ham from the tomatoes and carrots and peas and eating it.

Lucy opens the door on the driver's side of the car, gets in, slams the door, jumps out, and starts snatching children from the car and yelling, limp bodies piling on the yard between the car and Louise's trailer.

Louise overturns the trash bag on her way out the door, the image of the clock forever stopped on six staying in her head as she stumbles numb into the cold rain that does nothing to douse the fire inside.

"Sweet!" Lucy yells. "Hey, Sweet, call 911."

Sweet, on her porch, heads inside, slamming the door.

By the time Louise reaches the children, Lucy's boy and girl are moaning, sitting up, then bellowing, with Lucy screaming and the rain beating down on her broomed reddish hair. She kneels next to Little Angel and begins breathing into her mouth—breathing, listening, breathing—while the light from her yard grows brighter, a focal point for the straight-down rain. But Little Angel just lies there with her head cocked back and her eyes blank, rain soaking her green knit shirt and pants and those braids bound in machine-gum colored beads, mud-speckled.

Louise scoops her up, cradling and rocking her. "Baby, wake up," she says. "You be awright. You be awright. See, them other chirren awright." The child's head snaps back, exposing her tender brown throat.

The other children are screaming now, and people pour through the hedge. Bloop and Beanie and Roper seem to magically appear, solemn-faced and silent, watching Louise rock Little Angel in the rain. So much wailing all around, while the rain goes on as if nothing has changed since it started, or there is really no God up there after all to turn it off.

❖ ❖ ❖

The rain stops for the funeral on Sunday, at the white church on the south curve, sun kissing the tiny white casket going into the church, but the wailing goes on. Dreamer, Sweet, and Lucy, but not Louise. She never makes a sound, just cries inside where that fire still burns while the choir sings and the preacher preaches and a black woman in a white nurse's uniform fans Dreamer, right side, front row, courtesy of Homer's Funeral Home in Valdosta.

Louise, seated fourth row back from the front, left side, sits between Roper and Bloop. She can feel their eyes locked on her face—expecting what? Thinking what? That she will die now? That surely having lost Little Angel, Louise will die now. She lifts her navy straw hat from her head and sets it on her lap and turns it in her hands. Like a man would do. Like Wainer Taylor used to do. So many flowers for this child who hardly had shoes. So much time spent mourning this dead child who nobody had time for when she was alive. It's been almost a week since she died. Stretch white limousines and suits and dresses and that glossy white casket with brass handles, like a fancy jewelry box. Louise can't take her eyes off that. Can't take her eyes off the wispy girl in pink on the white satin display bed. Soon they'll be done. Soon she can sleep.

That night, Louise takes the scrapwork quilt, interfaced with burlap, and starts out the door of her trailer. "Granmama," says Bloop, watching TV, "where you off to?"

"Just out walking," she says.

Beanie in the chair by the door says, "It cold out there, Granmama."

"I be back," she says and shuts the door and goes down the doorsteps and across the moonlit yard, hearing Dreamer wailing inside her house as she passes in the flocked shadows of the oaks to the white sand road and the cemetery behind the white church. All white, even the headstones, with the moon riding high at midnight. Across the quarters, dogs bark and TVs blare, the juke throbs with its usual wild heartbeat. Walking among the graves, Louise sees Low's headstone and steps over his grave, saying, "We be just as dead as you," and on toward the raw dirt grave of Little Angel. She kneels at the grave and spreads the quilt over the mound and tucks it into the folds of chilled earth.

❖ ❖ ❖

With the money Roper has been handing over to Louise she has bought a hen, stewed it, and bogged it in corn-bread dressing for Thanksgiving dinner. While Roper and the boys watch the parade on TV—a calamity of music and scream talking—she slides the blue speckled pan into the oven and bakes it. When the chicken and dressing is browned to suit her, she takes it from the oven and sets it on the white Formica tabletop beneath the window overlooking the rain-pocked yard. Candied yams and turnip greens and giblet gravy leave barely enough space for the four white Melmac plates with wheat motifs, her train-wreck dishes.

Four days since the funeral and still Louise hasn't cried. At first, she'd vowed to quit keeping children, but when Monday came and the children came, she didn't say she wouldn't, so she just kept doing it till she knew she always would. At first, she'd vowed to give up her battle to make Roper into something, something good, but when she switched the shoe from dirty apron pocket to clean apron pocket, she knew she wouldn't do that either. At first, she vowed just to die, but when she didn't die, she knew she would have to live a while longer. And actually, as time started ticking again, she found herself even more eager to change the boys and Roper and the entire quarters. For Little Angel.

Yes, Louise is making progress. She is back on track; they all are. Even with the usual merry racket at Sweet's house across the hedge, Louise senses order in the quarters. Even figuring the funeral and the holiday combined will bring about more drinking and fighting and tomorrow the trash might be back along the road as before.

She unties her apron with the shoe in the pocket and hangs it on a hook behind the kitchen door. She has grown as used to the sag of the shoe as to her own breasts.

"Thanksgiving on the table," she calls and feet hit the living-room floor and bound toward the kitchen; Beanie, Bloop, and Roper flock like buzzards to the table.

As usual they are starving, but she makes them wait till she asks God's blessings, then gets up to turn off the TV. Thinking maybe she is pushing things a bit by refusing to let Bloop and Beanie carry their food-piled plates to the TV.

"Ain't nothing but news on, nohow," says Bloop and starts eating. Since Little Angel's death, Bloop and Beanie and Roper have been on their best behavior.

In the living room, hand on the power toggle of the portable TV, Louise watches an upclose clump of black children's faces gnawing on turkey legs—a day-care center in Philadelphia. And listens to a commentator's remarks on Deadbeat Dads and Single Moms—topics Louise knows well from the TV talk shows—mostly black. Sadness swells over her with the dawning realization that the black race is doomed when the scene switches to news of one black youth dousing another with gasoline and sticking a match to him. She turns them off. She can't take on the whole black race. She's not God.

❖ ❖ ❖

After dinner, Louise takes her apron from the hook on the kitchen door to cover her silky mauve church dress, and knows before she checks the pocket that the shoe is gone, Roper is gone. The boys are tussling in the living room, fighting over the remote control. Gazing out the window over the table, the picked chicken bones, she sees Roper slinking through the door of his trailer. She drops the apron and heads for the living-room door, passing through the din of TV-football racket unnoticed. Unnoticed, that is, until she starts hollering for Roper, and then the boys crowd in behind her and follow her hobbling down the doorsteps calling "Roper!" every breath. Across the yard, still hollering with the boys trotting after her.

She jerks Roper's trailer door open and stands there, locating him sitting in the chair by the door in the dull brown light.

"Give me that shoe," she yells and steps inside.

"What shoe that?" he says but doesn't look at her.

The boys stand outside the door, peeping in, as if they are watching a fight on TV.

"Bout the time I think you coming along," she huffs, holding her heart, "you turn back."

"You gone give yourself a heart attack, Mama," says Roper, now looking at her.

"Yeah, Granmama," says Bloop, stepping inside behind her. "Give her the shoe," he says to Roper.

"Yeah," says Beanie, "give her the shoe. We see you take it."

"Can't do it, Mama," says Roper. "I done clean up the whole quarters, work from daylight to dark, and hand over my money to you. You promise."

"I say by Christmas," she says and clutches her heart with her knobby hands. "I say tell Little Taylor what you know. You ain't did that yet, you ain't prove yourself yet."

"Granmama," says Beanie, taking her arm, "set down fore you fall down. Give her the shoe, Roper."

"Daddy," she corrects and jerks her arm away.

Roper snorts. "Them boys ain't studying me."

"He don't want nothing to do with us, Granmama," says Bloop and sits in a bowed metal chair at the table with his long legs apart. "Let him keep the shoe."

Roper sits forward. "I do all I can for y'all, but I ain't your mama."

"Granmama *my* mama," says Beanie and hooks his left arm about her shoulder. "Don't need no daddy," he says.

"Yeah," says Bloop, turning his cap around with the bill in front. "We ain't giving you no more trouble, Granmama. Are we, Beanie?"

"No ma'am," says Beanie.

For a truth, her heart is pounding, and she figures she must look ill, though she feels only mad, disheartened, sad about Little Angel. She wills herself pale, starts panting.

"Give me that chair, Roper," she says, wobbling toward him.

He shoots up and takes her right elbow and settles her into the chair. "Put your head down, Mama," he says. "You fixing to pass out, I didn't go to . . ."

"Now you done it, man," says Bloop, on his feet and ganging around her with the others.

"Oh, lordy me," says Louise with her head low. "Here I lose my Little Angel and . . ."

"Don't talk, Mama," says Roper. "Get her some water," he says to one of the boys.

"Don't talk, Granmama," says Beanie, sniffling now.

She starts sobbing and rocking, sobbing for real, for Little Angel, for all the Little Angels in the world, black and white. "That pore lil ole baby, pore lil ole throwed-away baby. We wait till she die then make a big to-do over her."

"She gone now, Mama," says Roper. "She with Jesus."

Bloop says, "Dreamer gone have you another one fore you know it, Granmama."

Louise sobs into her hands, her whole body shaking like a washing machine off balance. "Lord help us." She cries harder, now praying in earnest, a random outpouring. "Lord help us all and help Little Taylor in his misery on this fine Thanksgiving."

"He awright," says Roper. "Gone to drinking and riding round and all. Having a big time."

"Lord," she said, "don't nothing never change?" She cries. "Look like despite us having more money and freedom now, we worse off. Was happier picking plums along the roadsides, going to and from the commissary for food, money, and medicine. Back when the man there be over us."

Beanie starts, "I ain't seen no plums."

Roper butts in, "That ain't the point, boy. She trying to tell us we turn out sorry."

"What she want then?" asks Bloop.

"One thing I wanted fore I die, Lord," she says, "was to get all these chirren in the Christmas play at church."

"I be working on it, Mama," says Roper, kneeling before her. "I gone get em there."

"Yeah, Granmama," says Bloop, pressing a glass of water into her hand. "We hear him, didn't we, Beanie?"

"Granmama, he doing his dead-level best," says Beanie.

She sips water, thinking how all these years she's tried to act brave and well, and all it would have taken to set things in order was to act weak, sick, and wrecked.

"How many you got?" she says, holding her heart.

"How many what?" says Roper. "Younguns?"

She nods weakly.

"Got Sweet's for shore. Chuck swore he make his go, him and Walleyed Willie."

"Ain't but eight," she says, "need more." She rests her head on the chair back with her eyes on the rain-etched flowers of the ceiling tiles. "Need that little girl of Lorena's was setting on my lap other day."

Her head goes low, she cries, rocking and clutching her heart. But she is over mourning Little Angel and almost smiles because she might as well and if she doesn't smile now she will never smile again, and because they are all under her control again, at least for now. And if things change, no matter—she can feel the hard shoe under the foam chair cushion.

14

By the time the Freedom Riders arrived in the little turpentine camp, called Withers, in 1965, Louise had been so indoctrinated by Wainer with his *Tampa Tribune* news, about half of which she cared to read, that she had begun to half-believe in that symbolic equality for her people, as Wainer called them, but she never believed that her son and Wainer's son would become *their* sons. Equality and all the other itys and isms sounded good, though. And at Wainer's nudging, she was soon caught up in that cause she didn't really believe would work, like the churchy chant of her nationwide people, "I have a dream."

But in truth, at the beginning, she didn't want things to change in Withers. She had her own secret family, her son and his son and him, till Roper got beat up at the Alapaha bridge ("Mama Lou, Roper's bad hurt out here in my truck"), and the quarters burned, and only Louise had made good on her promise and registered to vote, and about one-fourth of Swanoochee County began to threaten Wainer and Math, calling them "nigger lovers." Then Louise wished she and her nigger son and nigger-loving husband and stepson could go back to the way they were, but there was nothing to go back to, because Wainer Taylor died when his pickup struck a pine tree, leaving Louise to walk blind through that fug of ideology that didn't pertain to her daily struggle in the quarters. *Freedom's not free.*

She couldn't even mourn Wainer openly at his funeral in the white church at Withers, which she attended as his housekeeper ("You can stand over here by the wall, Louise"), but it fired her up, a fire kindled out of anger then, and nostalgia later, under a guise of seeking equality for her people in the quarters that would literally burn before the summer ended. And with it the dream.

❖ ❖ ❖

Sometimes now the order of happenings from start to finish of that belated Freedom Summer in Withers gets jumbled on Louise's mind map: sounds of dogs barking or the whistle and rumble of a coming train spark memories of her running breathless in the fired dark from the quarters to the big house to tell Math Taylor that the quarters were burning. And then again, the smell of smoke ignites memories of Math Taylor coming to tell Louise that his daddy is dead, the order of things turning around on her, and only random chaotic or calm scenes coming clear as bought iceblocks.

Louise had been expecting a visit from some local whites when they came that late summer in 1965, or thought she had—she'd been warned by Wainer Taylor and the Freedom Riders. All gone then. But following Wainer's death and Roper's beating, she didn't see how anything worse could happen, though at the same time she felt that she wouldn't be surprised if something worse should happen.

From her cabin, where she was getting ready for bed, she could hear along the east curve of the quarters a sudden lone call like an owl hooting, followed by shouts and screams and broken talking and glass.

Passing through the dark front room, she could see firelight through the east window over Roper's bed, and the silhouette of his head lifted from his pillow. "What going on, Mama?" he said in that whipped voice that went with the newly whipped Roper, and she said, "Shh, just you lay there."

But going out the front door to the porch, she could hear him hopping after her and stop hopping just inside the screen door.

"Them ole mean boys be burning the quarters now," she said, sucking in her breath. "Come on."

Roper hopped out to the porch with his broken right foot held high; the white bandage around his head and the white cast on his foot gleamed in the burnished blackness. Louise hooked one arm around his waist and walked him down the doorsteps and around back, where already the fire from the east curve was blazing orange on the dirt and smoke like dust clouds was kicking up in the murky August sky.

"Where we going?" he said.

"Pappy's house."

"I can't make it that far, Mama," he said.

"Can't never could," she said, hurrying on through the yard behind her cabin, with him leaning heavy, past the lime-reeking outhouse, through the yards of other cabins, where people were knocking about and whispering inside, then stopping at the road in front of the white church with its cross spire and sighting up the orange strand of sand where women and children were scrambling from close-set burning cabins and screaming and men were thronging toward Ahab's place and knotting in the dark alley between a pickup and a two-ton truck loaded with fat gum barrels. Babies crying, dogs barking and lunging at flickering shadows.

"Come on," Louise said and hobbled with Roper through the churchyard, into the start of dense woods, where the fire from the quarters produced a queer shadowy light, like the midday sun during control-burning season, when smoke hovered over Withers. Across the wheel-polished rails of the tracks, she picked up the path her feet had tramped out over years of walking to and from Pappy's house since she left home to marry Low.

The spotty bleating and croaking of frogs pointed out the swampy places, left and right and ahead, as Louise and Roper passed from the lit section of woods and sounds of screaming and dogs barking, into the shrilling of katydids and strong darkness, like a wall they might walk into, and then the sudden sandy clearing of Pappy's yard, where his solitary red house stood out against the backdrop of more woods. No lights in the pieced-together house with green banisters along the front porch, but Louise could make out the swaying silhouettes of Pappy and his new wife and children and hear their scared whispering.

"It's me, Pappy," she said, "me and Roper."

"What they got going over there?" he called out in his excited little-man voice. He was old and timid now, but not too old and timid to still trap coons and women. Not too old and timid to love a little trouble.

"Hush up, Pappy!" she said low. "That them mean ole white boys beat up Roper at the river, I reckon."

She helped Roper up the tall, rickety doorsteps and

into the metal glider that trilled like a jaybird when she let go. "Stay here," she said to him and then to the others ganged around, "Pappy, y'all look out after him while I go for Little Taylor."

"You better look out," said Pappy, but she was off: across the open yard of sterile dirt and heading down the path, through bullous-vine tangles and switching gum branches and wax-berry myrtle bushes, cat-claw briers tearing at her legs and skirt to let her know when she strayed from the path.

The backlight of the tiered pines was higher, brighter, this side of the tracks, like the sun rising gold in the north, a strange tilt to Louise's world that could never be set right again. Her blue-sprigged skirt looked purple; the rails looked hot, like bars of smelting iron.

From the churchyard, she could see the string of burning houses along the north curve and flames lashing and backburning against the fire-stirred breeze toward the backs of houses facing the church. Only fire crackling, tin shrieking and wood groaning, and now and then glass snicking. No other sounds, no motion except for the flickering shadows on scorched dirt and rising fat-pine smoke that smelled peaceful as the ongoing fires of winter in the quarters' fireplaces.

Running breathless up the orange sand road to the highway, layered in smoke, she slowed to a walk along the still, darkened cabins fronting the narrow gravel road to the commissary and the big house, where a single light burned in the kitchen at the back. Wainer was dead. They had waited till Wainer was dead and the Freedom Riders had gone to set fire to the quarters. The cabins along the loop that hadn't yet burned would be burned

before she got back with Little Taylor, who was still nurs-
ing a broken heart from his daddy's death and a broken
nose from the fight at the river bridge where Roper was
beat up. She didn't really know who was burning the
quarters, but she suspected it was the same gang Roper
and Little Taylor had hired to work in tobacco, then
fired, then fought with. This time somebody might be
killed—somebody might already have been killed. If
Wainer was still alive, he would have been sent for right
away. She just hoped nobody had gone for Little Taylor,
and realized suddenly that was exactly what she was
doing—traipsing to the big house for the man. A habit
hard to break.

She turned around, walking. Walking straight up the
road to the highway, then the dirt road, toward the slow-
burning hoop of cabins with blackened clay-brick chimneys rising in the smoke-smeared sky like monuments to
the families who had lived there, through the yard of the
singed church with its white walls mirroring flames, and
on across the railroad tracks to her blazed path through
the woods, and Pappy's house that looked brighter red
than when she'd left. And there from the green-banis-
tered porch, under the cool green of camphor trees,
they watched the smoky glow across the woods and lis-
tened to the fire crackle and lash till the passing train
spelled their tired ears and eyes.

❖ ❖ ❖

Louise had been expecting the Freedom Riders too, but
when they came, alien on that ordinary June morning in
1965, she had already come to view them as the whole
symbolic cause, as turned around from the familiar as

was Wainer at times in his association with a black woman. But she loved Wainer, and she didn't love those white students in the blue car that parked first at the commissary and later in front of her cabin for all the world to see. High-mannered northern whites in her own cabin for two whole months, where having slept with a white man so long ago she'd forgotten he was white should have instilled some sense of familiarity with other whites.

The young man driving the car pulled up at the creosoted pine commissary that fine ordinary June morning and strolled over to where the black children were picking wild plums from the switches of trees along the commissary porch. Maybe it had been his voice when he said hello or maybe the way he was dressed in that black suit and white shirt and tie that sent the children skipping along the road to pick plums growing from the trees between cabins. Or maybe, like Louise, the children could smell trouble and believed if they kept enough distance they could avoid it.

The Freedom Riders could have stayed at the big house with Wainer—he'd invited them—but they opted to stay in the quarters with Louise and treated her and Roper white and Wainer and Math black for almost three months. Louise could tell right off that the girl named Annie and the others thought she was stupid. They'd come to make things right. To make right what wasn't wrong till they pointed out it was wrong.

Long days in the quarters now and, except for regular trips to the commissary, no Wainer, who was cheering Louise on from his office, where they kept council on occasion, but keeping his distance like the children, while Skinny Peter and Plain Annie ("Just call me plain Annie," she said, when Louise called her Miss because she didn't know her) and the others tracked over the barefoot prints of the quarters' roads with their smart city shoes, going house to house and urging everybody to register to vote. When they, the Freedom Riders, could catch somebody at home, that is. Which was seldom. Those who weren't working went to work, or slept right through the Freedom Riders' preacher-come-calling knocks on doors.

All except Old Ahab, who sat in a cowhide chair by the front door of his cabin, and said, "Yes um" and "No suh" and "I don't know," and grinned till his fat lips set up like concrete over his false teeth, but never moved from that chair by his door till rainy days, when he would shuffle on over to the open shed in the middle of the quarters and tighten hoops on gum barrels with his ballpeen hammer and tamp. While one of his boys, Ahab the Second or Third or maybe the Twentieth, spun the wooden barrels on the powdery gray dirt, and the spring rain pecked peacefully on the tin roof, Ahab would beat out a rhythm round and round the barrels, tamping down the metal hoops—great white teeth set in a grin and blue-ringed brown eyes pinned on the sole task appointed to him by Wainer, who was rapidly taking on the role of token Southern white landowner and therefore suspect, according to the passed-down, prescribed Yankee standards of the Freedom Riders.

Time out from his task, and the rain picked up Old Ahab's rapping rhythm, with the frogs' blatting from the wet green woods and now and then a blacksnake cheeping, trying to fool birds into believing it was only a baby chick. Old Ahab leaned brittlely left and hooked his right thumb in the handle of a plastic jug of clear, boiling shine and lifted it to his poked-out lips and took a swig. Wiped his mouth on the sleeve of his blue shirt and flashed his fine white teeth.

"What's in the jug, Mr. Ahab?" asked Skinny Peter, stepping out of the crowd gathered to watch like folks at an arts-and-crafts show. He had a goatee, wet-black as his curly hair. His mouth twitched continuously as if a string were attached to the right corner.

"Shine—hunderd proof." Old Ahab raised the jug proudly then reset it closer to the round black kettle where hogs were scalded each winter and cane juice was cooked each fall.

"You mean like illegal whiskey, right?"

Old as the roll of ages, Old Ahab cackled and set his eyes on the cluster of barrels, one wheeling his way, between hand-hewed poles supporting the shed.

"You the revenue man?" he said.

"No revenue man," said Skinny Peter and pocketed his hands in his blue jeans. Sometimes he wore sandals. Sometimes canvas deck shoes—white with sopped-dirt soles today.

"Bossman, he allays give he hands a jug apiece, end of the work week." Old Ahab reached up with his huge hands and grabbed the lip of the wooden barrel and helped Little Ahab wrest it to the ground like one of the wild pineywoods rooters fattening in the pen across the wire fence. The razor-backed hogs had been lured to the scrub post in the woods—a single pole wrapped in oil-sopped croaker sacks to kill lice and fleas. Old Ahab and his boys clipped rings in the noses of their hogs to prevent them from rooting up troughs of water and shorts, a gruel of corn husks soaked in water, and cut out the nuts of the boars to make them grow faster and to rid the pork of its strong taste. Old Ahab had explained all this to the Yankees and explained how he and his boys notched the ears of the hogs with Taylor's swallowfork and underbit mark, a V and an upside-down U, to show ownership. But somehow the hard-headed Yankees had turned that around to mean that Ahab and his boys had risked their lives to furnish Taylor with wild meat for his table.

"Mr. Wainer know he can't do without me," said Ahab—RAP RAP RAP TING.

"Is that how this Taylor guy pays his labor, with illegal whiskey?" asked Plain Annie, standing next to Peter with her thin, moley arms crossed.

Old Ahab didn't answer right off, just kept eyeing the spinning barrel for gaps between staves, rapping round with his hammer till he spotted the sucker, while his boy jigged, a bit stiff and self-conscious and conveniently deaf. Suddenly: "No um, Bossman pay he labor fair and square," Old Ahab spoke up, no foolishness on that ancient face, whose catface image he had carved on countless crops of turpentine timber in the flatwoods for half a century.

"Bossman, he take us to the doctor in Valdosta when we sick," Old Ahab preached, pounding out each syllable with his hammer and tamp like a gavel. "He take us to the tooth dentist when we needs more teeth; he go to the judge when we in trouble; he make sho we have shoes on our feet and meat in our smokehouse, and ery man beat up on his wife better look out for the bossman cause he can wind up daid."

"You mean Taylor actually kills men who abuse their wives?" one of the Freedom Riders asked.

"I ain't say no more." Old Ahab wagged his white head and rapped his way around another barrel with his hammer. "Y'all run on now," he said, shooing them like children from under his feet—those carefully tied old brogans. "Louise want y'all to know what went with Low, she tell you," he added.

"Mr. Ahab"—Skinny Peter waved Annie back—"we didn't come here to insult your way of life, we just . . ."

"See that fellow walking there," Old Ahab butted in, keeping his all-seeing eyes on the barrel before him and tamping down a hoop without letup.

They all turned, while Old Ahab kept talking, and watched a wiry black man in black rubber boots walking briskly in the rain around the north curve, where unpainted cabins bermed the road, colorless as the mud. Neat green garden squares, between cabins, with yellow crookneck squash and red ripe tomatoes. Still rockers on front porches since the Freedom Riders came to Withers. "That be Walter Edmund, come from up there at Mr. Bee gum camp," said Old Ahab. "Bossman pay off what he be owing to Mr. Bee and put him to tacking turtentine tins on this here place bout six month ago. Go ast Edmund what he know."

"Taylor *bought* him?" said Skinny Peter.

"Bossman ain't *buy* nobody," said Old Ahab—*rap rap rap ting*—and gazed mean at them in his humble bib overalls.

❖ ❖ ❖

"You work for this Taylor guy?" Plain Annie asked Louise one hot morning in her kitchen.

"In a way I do," Louise said and dumped the scrambled eggs from the blue bowl into the puddle of bubbling butter in her black iron frying pan. On a white wood shelf above her white stove stood a red valentine from Wainer, signed with a kiss only she could see. She cut her eyes back to watch Plain Annie in her blue plaid Bermudas and white blouse and loafers settle onto the high wood stool to watch Louise, who stood barefoot in a red seersucker shift that framed her unbound breasts, her squeezed waist, and flared hips. Long planed legs and trim ankles, but splayed feet. *Law, gal! What your mama mean naming you Louise when you look like Cleopatra? All except for them feet.*

"Does he pay you well?" asked Annie.

"He do," said Louise and lifted the gelling eggs with a spatula to let the wet yellow slide to the bottom of the pan.

"May I ask how much?"

Louise didn't answer, had found she didn't have to answer, and that not answering was the key. But what she'd have liked to tell Annie was, You don't understand; tend to your own damned business.

"My guess is," said Annie, changing from pointed to polite, "you don't have a social security number. I've yet to meet anybody here with a social security number."

Louise could feel her face heating up like the sun through the south window over her cook table. "I have me a social security number, been and had one going on five year."

"Surprise!" said Annie and twirled around on the stool with her small brown shoes out. "Any man who beats his labor with a gin belt tacked to a wooden paddle must be too busy to bother with social security."

"Somebody be pulling your leg." Louise laughed and wheeled to face the young woman with the round girl face and freckles. That dead brown hair cooped at her collar. "Wainer Taylor ain't beat nobody. He tar and feather a bunch though. You know how tar hold in body heat so you can't sweat, skin can't breathe. Man run out on his wife can look out for Wainer Taylor to tar his privates, sprinkle some chicken feathers on him, and hang him from a pole by his wrist and feets and tote him through the quarters for the whole world to see."

Annie's narrow brown eyes stretched, had been stretching since Louise began the story, then stared down at her lap as if she suspected Louise was the one pulling her leg. And was sorry maybe that she had forced such a sorry story.

"Go tell them others get up, I got breakfast," Louise said, dismissing her.

"We don't mean to keep you in the kitchen like this, Mrs. Rackard," said Annie. "We could go out to eat."

"*Out* be a good thirty mile from here. I ain't above cooking." Louise dunked the hot skillet in the dishpan of water. She'd never seen so many houseflies—on the cook table, the eating table, the window screens—humming like a harmonica. Usually, by late June, the unpainted tongue-and-groove walls of her cabin would be white-washed with DDT, but the Freedom Riders had gagged and griped about the smell, said Taylor was trying to kill them all by ordering one of the hands to spray the quarters regularly. Let the flies and mosquitoes eat them up, Louise decided. She had quit feeling self-conscious about this house she hardly lived in and started hoping if the Freedom Riders became uncomfortable enough, they would leave. The eggs were getting cold.

"How old is your son Roger?" asked Annie.

"Roper," said Louise and stirred the grits she knew they wouldn't eat.

"What happened to Roper's father?"

"Low get kill in a sawmill muckup," she said and carried the eggs to the long wooden table with two benches.

"An accident, huh?" said Annie.

"That right."

"One of your neighbors told a different story."

"People always telling stories round here," said Louise.

Louise waited till Annie tapped from the room, then left through the humming of flies on the porch, where the bucket on the water shelf sat empty, accusing.

All along the road between the quarters loop and the commissary, dark-skinned children were playing and laughing. When Louise passed, they eyed her and stopped laughing and skipped behind the side-by-side shotgun houses, where wine-stemmed bushes of Thorny Careless grew from the snuff-rich dirt. Ferny fronds of the mimosa trees were putting on airy pink flowers like the crests of peacocks' heads.

She walked faster, truly mad now. Locusts keening in the surrounding woods like the blood in her ears, and the far-off fractured pinging, whining, and buzzing of the sawmill. Sounds of midday, midsummer. She could hear the men chipping and dipping, in the various drifts of the turpentine woods: the intermittent *schlp schlp* of pine

bark slicing under the chippers' hacks; and the knocking ring of iron paddles on metal buckets to loosen the
dipped gum, then deeper and more vigorous, the dip-
pers' paddles banging on their bucket bottoms to signal
another bucket dumped into the barrel.

Sights and sounds of summer so different from the
other seasons: the woodpecker rapping of hammers tacking turpentine tins onto pine trunks, in late winter and
spring, and the linking hoots of the hands calling out
their names for the woodsrider to credit them with
another tin set. Another tin set to receive the slow run of
summer resin. All about the woods, the rectangular tin
cups could be seen shining in contrast with the burned
straw and brush from the control burning of late fall and
winter—scraping time, streaking time. So different and
yet the same, the sights and sounds of each season, still
work without letup, the business of turpentine.

The sky today was clear blue and the sun white, show-
ering straight down, while the Freedom Riders were just
eating breakfast.

"Nosy, lazy bunch of good-for-nothings," Louise mumbled and stepped from the grassed shoulders of the
gravel road to the sandy rake-marked yard of the creosoted commissary, where a new green pickup was
parked before the porch. Usually if someone was inside
the commissary Louise would either turn around, go
home, and come back later, or go on in and wander the
dim musty aisles between tall shelves of canned vegetables and meats and staples until whoever—generally
some man from the community stopping by just to jaw
and swig on a cold drink—got talked out and left.

But this time she marched up the brittle board

doorsteps to the sunny half porch with plank benches nailed post to post. The motor of the meat case inside loaded the hot air with more humming and Wainer Taylor's elevated monotone, mixed with the deal-of-a-lifetime voice of another man. Smells of cottonseed meal and tobacco wafted through the open vertical-board door set in the walled-in north end of the porch. In the doorway Louise stopped, sun-blinded, and when at last she could see, she was locking eyes with Wainer Taylor, who sat slumped on a wooden stool with his long legs spraddled behind the carved-on mahogany counter. He sat up straight, lit aqua eyes beaming. "Louise!" he said.

A short, stocky man in a sky-blue suit and yellow shirt stood on the other side of the counter with his back to Louise. He turned around, measuring her with watery blue eyes, a cigar stuck between his thick, raw lips. He turned again, facing Wainer, and went on talking, with his lardy body supported by one elbow on top of the counter and a short, fat leg wedged against the counter wall.

Louise walked on through the open space, where four cowhide-bottomed chairs and a black iron stove sat in a block of sun from the barred south window. Black strips of flypaper twirled from strings attached to the raftered ceiling, where a paddle fan whirred. Dust specks drifted and turned in the sun funnels produced by the window bars. She could tell Wainer had just swept the wide plank floors because of the flying dust, and she could tell he was trying to wrap up his conversation by the way he scuffed his boots on the floor and talked louder.

The man shifted his weight, the floor creaked, but he kept standing in the same spot till Wainer strolled around the counter and walked and talked him out the door.

In a few minutes, Wainer was back, stepping from the sunny spot to the cool, dim aisle where Louise stood waiting at the other end.

"I-God!" he said, walking toward her. "Old truck salesman, trying to talk me into trading. Got to where they try anything to get you to buy something—wanting to leave me that new pickup he's riding in and drive my old one back to town. All I have to do is sign the papers, he says."

Between the shelved corned beef and canned tomatoes, he changed tones. "Law, gal," he said low and cackled, "I been missing you."

"Don't you *law gal* me," she said, strolling on around a bank of sacked sugar and flour toward his office at the back of the commissary, with him following. "Shut the door," she said when he stepped in behind her.

He shut the door and stood behind her with his sandpapery hands on her level shoulders and his thorny beard on her crane neck. "You missing me, ain't you, gal?" he said.

She wheeled, stared into his squinched aqua eyes. "How come you didn't just tell the man I be your common-law wife?"

"Cause he wadn't worth telling who you are to me?"

"You know what I mean."

"Okay," he said, holding out both hands. "Next time you come in the store and somebody's here, I'll make like I don't see you. I'll shut my eyes and my mouth. That make you happy?"

"I ain't happy, ain't never gone be happy till them Yankees go back where they come from. I be sick and tired of playing up to a bunch of school younguns out looking for something to get into."

"Now, Louise," Wainer said and sat on his paper-piled desktop and crossed his arms. "They doing this for the right reason, I reckon. Or maybe they just practicing up."

"Well, let em go practice somewhere else. Evertime I turn around, they be picking. Bout ready to hang you and me both over Low."

"Nobody must of not told em how Low and his buddy Simmy axe-slaughtered that old Negro man and woman over round Cornerville for a dollar or two. Hadn't been for her throwing hot grease in Simmy's face, the law wouldn't of tracked him down and took him in neither. Old dogs was lapping up the grease when their girl youngun come by and found her mammy and pappy dead on the dirt floor. Heard a while back they let Simmy go, said he was what they call rehabilitated now. He just better not come rehabilitating round here's all I gotta say."

"Them Freedom Riders would say let the law handle such," said Louise with her pouty lips thinning the way they did when she got mad. "Say that what the law for."

"Tell em bout the law coming out that time Low broke your jaw for sassing back, tell em bout the time Low kicked you in the belly and you having a baby. Tell em bout the law saying, 'That's just niggers fighting for you!'"

"Shoot," she said, black eyes rolling in her oval face. "I ain't tell em nothing. Here it be dinnertime and them still laying up and me making breakfast. I be wore out from hearing bout voting."

"Come here, gal," he said and she automatically slipped into his firm arms, between his firm legs, her long, slim arms looping around his neck—sweat and tobacco and soap.

He patted her back and held her. "See, gal, a cause is like that. They's people in it and people can't make it perfect like it is on paper. Like it sounds. We all just flesh and blood when it comes right down to it. Eating, drinking, sleeping, and loving."

"They treating me like a nigger cook, then making like cooking for white people's the worst thing in the world. They the ones pointing out who be black and who be white."

"Won't be long now," he said, rubbing her back and breathing hard. "Won't be long and me and you'll pick up where we left off."

He lifted her bushy blunt hair and kissed her neck, her right ear. "They've about wore my telephone out, calling home, then treat me like I'm the one started the Civil War they been studying in school. If I could fix everthing where it'd be even-steven, don't you reckon I would?"

"They just don't understand us and our ways," she breathes into his face. "How much longer you reckon they'll stay?"

"Another week or so," he said and kissed her cheek, her mouth. "Then they'll be gone."

"If they don't . . . ?"

"Tell em about us and come on home."

"That Annie would die!" Louise laughed. "She'd say you just using my body."

He laughed. "I am."

❖ ❖ ❖

First of August and the Freedom Riders were still kicking about the quarters and taking over church meetings on Sundays. Everybody was getting used to them, and even chanted and sang their freedom songs, while batting the hot, sticky air with hand fans. First thing on Monday they would register to vote, yes sir, but Monday mornings would find them back in the turpentine woods, chipping and dipping, and the Freedom Riders back at the commissary or the big house, blaming Wainer for making them work, or shanghaiing the pickup loads of hands coming home for dinner. "Yessir, tomorrow we sho nuf go vote."

"No, *register*, we want you to register to vote in the next election."

Louise's butter beans and peas were just coming in and she put Annie to picking and shelling—give her something useful to do—and even taught her to cook, though God knew, if not for Louise, the vegetables wouldn't be fit to eat. That's what Louise would tell Wainer when she went to the big house to take sliced red tomatoes and cucumbers, stewed yellow squash and mixed butter beans and peas, with hamhocks, cornbread, and fried chicken wings.

"Yo mama must-a pack that shirt away for a keepsake," she said, greeting him in the hollow green hallway with her cardboard box of food.

He gazed down at the snug brown plaid shirt and brushed his hands across his broad chest and flat stomach, where a white T-shirt peeped between the tugged buttons of the placket. Then he laughed and slapped her backside. She dodged him, laughing too, and headed up the hall toward the sitting room, with its low, sloped ceiling. His brown vinyl recliner was covered in *Tampa Tribune*s, with an electric floor fan blowing and rattling them.

"You make me spill these peas and butter beans and I let you starve," she said, "hard as they be to pick."

"I know how to batch," he said, following her. "Don't need no woman now. I done overed needing women."

She walked on through the sitting room to the narrow smoked-green kitchen on the northeast end of the house and set the box of stacked bowls and platters on the white counter between the stove and sink, then followed the brown trail of scuffed green linoleum between the length of cabinets and the bar. She opened the heavy wood door, letting out the stale air and letting in the warble of wrens, the green smell of cut grass and oakmoss, and the piercing white light of the centering August sun. Across the oak-shady grassed yard, beyond the bleached and drying corn patch, Louise could see Annie on the front porch of the nearest cabin, talking to a woman who was peeling pears into a dull aluminum pan on her lap.

Somehow Annie had stopped prying for answers to the big questions and started begging answers to the little questions, such as how to tell a huckleberry from a blueberry, and wrote Louise's answers on a yellow steno pad and read them back to be sure: "Huckleberries are hazy blue, grow on high bushes, and have bigger leaves than blueberry bushes. Blueberries and gallberries are both ink-blue, though gallberries are bitter and only robins eat them. Blueberries have fluted openings, like a second skin."

Same with Old Ahab: posted on his porch at his feet, Annie wrote while he grumbled about the swamps being cleared and the woods being opened up by the loggers, who were messing up the creeks and branches. Ditches no longer contained pop-bellied minnows to eat up the skeeter eggs. How come the dern skeeters be eating us up, he said. What, Annie asked Louise, are skeeters?

Wainer pulled out a wooden stool and sat at the end of the bar nearest the sitting room, with his long legs in faded denim stretched to the white stove, and watched Louise unpack the food.

"Peas," he said. "Law, gal, my mama used to pick em, shell em, blanch em, put em up every summer. Then after her stroke, the doctor put her to picking up one pea at a time and passing each from bowl to bowl. For therapy. I've thought about that many's the time. Seems to me like a woman ain't nothing but a slave to her family."

"Men too," said Louise. "Work like dogs to feed a family, put a roof over their heads. End up slumped in a chair with their tongues lolling when they get old."

"Them that don't work ends up the same way."

She spun around and cut her great black eyes at him. "What got you so down and out today?"

"Ah, ain't nothing a good fishing trip wouldn't cure."

"Then go fishing. Get that boat out yonder under that shed and set it floating on the river."

"Takes faith to fish, gal." He wenched his right booted foot onto his left knee, lifting his chin and his voice. "But that old Alapaha does beckon. So quiet and clean you hate to leave trash or noise."

Uh oh! This festering black melancholy was about to erupt and expose a cancer if Louise didn't stop it. "Ain't showing no sign of leaving, them Yankees," she said and took from the box a cake of cornbread wrapped in a blue towel. "That Annie making herself useful, though."

"I figgered you'd take a shine to em if they hung around long enough."

"Huh!" she said and gave him a sidelong glance, then set a pot of water on the stove to boil for tea. "I ain't never taking a shine to nobody bad-mouth you. Always hounding you bout stuff ain't nobody even think about before they come."

"Do you good," he said. "But they bout quit harping on the little stuff, seen it wadn't getting em nowhere, I reckon. Doing what they come here to do in the first place. But I ain't making nobody go register to vote don't want to, and I told your Yankees that. Well, maybe Roper. I'm making Roper register to vote tomorrow." His smoke-razed monotone rose. "If they'd just listen to theirselves, they'd hear all kinds of contradictions."

"Well, don't take it out on me."

"You right," he said low. "I just don't like them worrying you."

"Oh, we get along." She set the bowl of mixed beans and peas with hamhock chunks on the bar. "Me and Annie, we get along."

"Come on now, you know you like that lil ole gal."

"She grow on you."

"Cute lil old gal, ain't she?"

"Wormy. Bout got bear-caught picking butter beans this morning."

He laughed. "Maybe you feeding them too good's how come they're staying."

"Feeding em like regular company," she said. "Little Taylor and Roper stay at the baccer barn again last night?" Louise set the bowl of stewed yellow squash next to the peas and beans, then the platter of fried chicken wings to one side.

"Yes ma'am," he said, crossing his arms. "They still firing that old wood barn. Got it cleaned up and wed around like a playhouse. Would shore tickle my daddy if he was alive to see our boys using that log barn he built."

"Make them eat if they come in." She took a chipped rock of clear ice from the freezer, set it in the white pan by the sink, and started picking ice and dropping chunks into two tall glasses.

"Law, gal, they ain't gone starve. Been back and forth to the commissary for cold drinks and soda crackers and Vienna sausage."

"Ain't good for them," she said, wiping her hands on a dish towel. "Dodging the Yankees is what they doing."

He laughed and squared his body to the bar and folded his long legs underneath. "Gone sell their first cooking of tobacco next Wednesday, and I want you to knock off from what you doing and go with me to the sale."

"I got company, man," she said and took two white plates with scalloped borders from the cabinet over the side-set window, where a glass rooster toothpick holder and a dish of dirty soap sat on the sill. Ah, the cancer.

Silence, while the locusts in the oaks beyond the back screen door droned on. While the crickets clicked in the patch of drying cornstalks between the big house and the next cabin over, heaviest and best ears of corn tipping toward the ragweed-rich dirt.

"They gone be hurt if you don't go to the sale, Louise, and it their first big money-making venture."

She turned serious. "Don't even ask me, Wainer. You know I want to go, and you know I be glad in my heart you give the boys that old Mahaffy place to grow their baccer on."

"No *give* to it," he said, sampling the dark bean liquor

with his spoon while she wasn't looking. "I rented it to them just like anybody else. They got to pay me back for fertilize and all too.

"Hired a bunch of boys from down there in Cornerville won't half work," he added.

"Well, don't say nothing," she said, "let em learn the hard way."

"I ain't . . . I ain't fixing to. I'm gone make myself scarce till the sale. I got woods to ride thi'safternoon anyhow. But I did tell them how to color sandlugs to where it'd look like pure gold and bring top dollar."

"How's that?"

"Told them to sprinkle sulfur on the wood flues and run slow heat a couple of days."

"Ain't nothing wrong in telling em stuff like that." She placed both glasses of tea on the white Formica bar and sat on the stool next to him.

He reached for her left hand and squeezed it. "I want you back, gal, I want you home. And I want you with me when the boys sell their tobacco next week. You can ride on back of the truck like a dog if you want to."

"Eat, man," she said and laughed and took her hand back.

He started eating. "Ain't nothing like good summer squash," he said. "But they bout gone now, ain't they?"

"Sandspurs taking over," she said, "what the worms ain't got into."

"That's the way of it," he said, "how it's supposed to be. But I tell you, if you want to get shed of sandspurs you have to pluck them up by hand and burn them."

"That must be something like your whistling to make the wind blow," she said and smiled.

The kitchen bloomed with the clean strong smell of steeped tea; a clock ticked from Wainer's high-ceilinged bedroom up the hall. He didn't smile, just stared down at his cornbread sopped with bean liquor.

She bit into a cucumber wedge and stared ahead at the calendar on the green tongue-and-groove wall. "Wainer, you gotta quit this trying to make me go places with you. Ain't doing nothing but messing with my head. I can't go and you know I can't go."

He drank from his glass of tea and shook his ice. "I know it, I just don't understand it. A man loves a woman, he wants her with him." He set the glass down hard and spoke up. "We got boys together, woman."

He stopped talking, with his stiff fingers latched around the glass, and Louise followed the lead of his eyes to the backdoor and Annie's shocked pale face behind the screen like a picture having hung there forever that you've just noticed.

❖ ❖ ❖

If Louise had known that would be the last time she would see Wainer, she would have stayed; if she had known that evening he would drive his pickup into a pine, she would have taken his truck key. She would have stopped death.

But while Peter and Annie and the others were seated around her kitchen table that night, studying road maps and talking about Florida—they were going to Florida!— Louise was putting fresh sheets on the beds and pallets for them to sleep and believing that tomorrow she and Wainer would pick up where they left off before the Freedom Riders came and she might even go with him to the tobacco sale next Wednesday because now that Annie knew about them and hadn't mentioned it, and the world hadn't blown up, Louise was feeling like somebody with a right.

But then she heard Little Taylor's bad-news voice behind the front screen door, calling her low, and she snapped another crisp white sunned sheet to block the sound because she knew in her heart that when she walked from the bedroom to the living room and heard what Little Taylor had to say and came back to finish putting sheets on the beds she wouldn't be entertaining thoughts of going anywhere with Wainer and felt almost relieved, a feeling that kept her from from buckling under from what she didn't yet know but knew would change them all forever.

"Mama Lou," he called again and knocked on the door so that it frammed in its frame, and she stopped snapping the sheet and clutched it to her chest like a bandage over her heart and crept from the cramped side room to the front room and faced Little Taylor behind the screen door. Just a smile, dear Lord, just let him be smiling.

"What?" she said and stopped walking, just stood under the hanging bare bulb, where night beetles swirled, and tried to read that sunburned sad face behind the gray mesh screen.

He stepped inside and closed the door easy and walked the long walk of the bad-news bearer to the center of the room and wrapped both arms around her, rocking, then led her to the couch and sat with her. "Daddy's dead, Mama Lou," he choked out.

"What you mean dead?"

"He had a truck wreck thi'sevening. On his way to see me and Roper at the baccer barn. Died a while ago in the hospital in Valdosta."

She buried her face in the sheet, stifling crying, hoping when she looked again Little Taylor would be grinning, would say he was just teasing. He teased her all the time, but never about bad things.

"Where they got him now?" she said because she needed a picture to go with her loss. She lowered the sheet to her lap.

"Up yonder at the funeral home."

"Valdosta."

"Yes ma'am, till the funeral." He choked out the last part.

Louise pulled him to her, longing to tell him she loved Wainer Taylor, that Wainer Taylor loved her, but instead said to Annie, standing stricken in the kitchen doorway with a biscuit in her right hand, "Y'all go on now," then going away herself to stay at the big house, where she would wait till two in the morning to slip into Wainer's room, into Wainer's bed, and sniff the sharp-sweat smell of his pillow, and cry.

Strangely, after the funeral, it was Annie that Louise told the whole story because Louise had to tell somebody and Annie already knew the ending and was leaving anyhow, and it was Annie who said she understood and wrote letters to Louise saying she understood till she wrote herself into true understanding.

15

Sunday evening, while the cold sun lowers over the quarters, torching the broomsage patch, children by the dozens straggle toward the white board church on the south straightaway to the highway. Even the older girl who looks pregnant. A surefire Mary. Beanie will be Joseph, though he doesn't know it yet. Perfect.

Supported by the two boys, one on each side lifting up on her elbows, Louise hobbles through her sun-glazed yard, through her collard patch, coming out in the backyard of Dreamer's west-side neighbor Lorena, who is standing with one hip cocked on her trashy front porch facing the church. Fussing with Roper, standing on the road.

"Ain't no law say that baby gotta be in no play," she says.

"*Law* what it gone be," says Roper, "if you don't get your ass out there looking for that youngun." He points east toward the curve where the juke is revved up for the end of the weekend. Where a wanton band of children are playing and squealing.

"You ain't have nothing on me," Lorena shouts, waddling across the porch toward the open door exhibiting more trash.

"Shit I ain't!" he says and spies his mama and the boys hobbling around the side of the house and switches to nice: "How you feeling, Mama?" he says to Louise and pockets his wildly gesturing hands.

Feebly she stands tall and eyes the children and dogs moiling in the churchyard across the road. "No good atall," she says and hangs her head, watching her black lace-up shoes inch across the footprinted dirt of Lorena's front yard. "Tell her I see her buying crack from the fish man last week," she whispers to the boys.

She has to repeat, speaking up in a weak, trembly voice, for Bloop to hear and rerepeat for Roper and Lorena to hear.

Lorena, about to go through the door, where a big fire burns in the fireplace and a baby cries, huffs down the doorsteps, mumbling, and heads around the curve toward the juke.

Cold shadows stripe the dirt before the shadowy inset church porch, the boy children tussle and shove and fuss, dogs bark, and Louise steps into the crowd, already picking out children to match the characters in the Christmas play. The wise men wander off around the twin sweetgums, with a plank bench nailed trunk to trunk, toward the railroad track behind the church, but Roper hazes them back, grumbling low and grimacing.

The bright-skinned Baptist preacher in Catholic-priest garb stands on the boxy church stoop waving his arms at the children and dogs, now parting for Louise to be paraded through the crowd. Slow up the steps and then settling like a queen in the chrome-legged chair by the door. Waiting for the star of the play.

In a few minutes, Lorena comes sashaying up the road from the juke with the new little angel skipping behind, braids bobbing in the slant of late sun. Lorena angles off toward her house, mumbling, and Roper crosses the road and takes the child by the hand and leads her through the crowd to Louise. Louise lifts the child to her lap, and bounces her on her knees with the black pocketbook and Lora Taylor's shoe wedged between them.

"Let em on in," she says to the preacher.

The preacher opens the church door to the hazy red light produced by the setting sun through red curtains, that sanctified, set-aside silence of mold, dust, and mice and the Holy Ghost. The children begin filing into and filling up the old slat-pine pews, which have seldom been so rocked and knocked and buffed by warm bodies. Must be fifty children with Roper bringing up the rear, like a prison guard, and then Miss Louise and Beanie and Bloop ambling up the aisle to the plyboard altar. The holy church brimming with unholy racket.

"Y'all shut up!" yells Roper, facing the children with his back to the altar, where Bloop and Beanie are depositing their grandmother in one of the high-backed chairs against the choir loft.

The boys start to leave her and she grabs Bloop's arm and in a sickly whisper tells him to go tell his daddy to run down to the juke and tell Sweet she'll have to come play the piano. Louise's usual job, in addition to Sunday-school teacher, secretary and treasurer, and janitor. Bloop looks at his grandmother sidelong but legs down from the platform, talking to Roper, who shakes his head and slaps his right leg. He steps forward, whispering to his mama. "Ain't gone work, Mama," he says. "Besides, Sweet can't play worth a shit."

"Watch it!" she says, watching the preacher walk between them, then holds her heart.

Whether Roper has taken her to mean "watch your mouth in front of the preacher" or "watch out you don't give me a heart attack," he is off, spring-walking up the aisle and out the door.

When Louise has just about given up hope of Sweet coming to play the piano—or, for that matter, even Roper coming back—she has gone too far this time—in walks Roper with his hand latched around one of Sweet's muscled brown arms, as if he is arresting her. She is puffed up, mad and splendid in shiny pink tights and tunic, the one with tangled gold snakes, and that long fat braid down her back, a blister of red for a mouth. She yanks away from Roper, but rollicks toward the splintered-veneer piano at rest along the west wall, where the red sun is withdrawing.

Louise, weak-eyed, surveys the children with runny noses tossing song books and Roper fussing and Sweet wildly beating the keys of the old piano—"Silent Night"—and feels she has indeed taken on the whole world.

The sky is just losing its blue hue when they start for home, Louise between the two boys, shortcutting across yards, and Roper a few steps ahead, almost to the collard patch. In the west, a quarter moon cradles the evening star. The whooping of children freed from church arches with the dusk over the quarters. A rooster crows, dogs bark. Sour smells of dishwater dashed out of doors and overflowing septic tanks. The usual, but something else. Someone else.

Roper stops, pockets his hands, and starts whistling.

Louise and the boys step up and stand beside him and

stare at the white Chevy pickup blocking the gap in the hedge, at the white man sitting on Louise's doorsteps with his head hung and his elbows propped on his knees.

"Little Taylor," she says and starts walking.

He looks up, then down as if his head is heavy.

"I tole you he be drinking," whispers Roper.

"Hush!" Louise says. "Take them boys to your trailer. Tell em stay there till I say come home."

Roper sighs, sucks in, and turns to the boys, whispering.

Pocketbook hooked on her elbow, Louise walks toward the doorsteps, trying to lift the downcast eyes with her own eyes. She's never quite overed being afraid of drunks, but she's not afraid of this one. Just sad.

"Look who come to see me," she says, so close she can smell the whiskey. His stale clothes.

"Mama Lou," he says, head rising like a bubble in water. "I'm messed up, Mama Lou." His head drops. His belly hangs between his parted legs. Dirty blue jeans, muddy boots. Blue chambray shirt minus two bottom buttons.

She places one hand on his right shoulder. "What business you got being by yo'self and it Thanksgiving?" She seems to be fussing with herself, and he lets her.

In a minute: "They ain't found her, Mama Lou," he says. "Ain't fixing to find her, looks like."

"Hush, now," she says, rubbing his fleshy back. "I got collards and hamhocks waiting on the stove with a pone of cornbread."

He stands up, unbogs his belt from his bloated waist. "I can't eat, Mama Lou. I gotta go." He staggers toward his truck, stumbles; she steps behind, turns him, and steers him toward the doorsteps again. No resistance.

Inside, she switches on the living-room light and then the kitchen light, and takes his arm and leads him to the scoured white sink, turns on the water, and sets his hands beneath the flow. Pours dish detergent into his hands, and while he washes and rinses she wets a bleached dish rag and takes off his cap and mops his sick-white face that extends over the top of his head. Gray curls that used to be blond.

"How long you be like this?" she says.

He steps back, holding to the counter edge, with his face down for her to wipe. "Feels good, Mama Lou. Thank you."

His eyes are closed and she doesn't realize he is crying till tears begin dripping to the white tile floor. No more words. She leads him to the table and pulls out a chair, and he sits, swaying side to side under the white light that makes him whiter, her blacker.

She starts to fix him a plate of collards and cornbread, but instead opens a can of chicken-noodle soup and dumps it into a pan and heats it. The pan sings while he cries low. Then she pours the soup into a white bowl and opens a pack of saltine crackers and sets it all before him. He eats slow, then fast, his pale aqua eyes touching her. "I ain't like this all the time," he says, "I want you to know that."

"Ain't nobody blame you if you was."

He smiles. "My daddy used to say, 'Ain't nothing ails you so bad Louise can't fix it. Her castor oil don't do it, her cooking will.'"

"That Campbell soup you eating, boy." She laughs. Sits across from him. "Yo daddy sho be good to me and

Roper," she says, watching his face, wondering what he knows, how much he knows. She can't tell.

Silence while the wind stirs in the chinaberry tree. A screen door slams.

"Truth is, Mama Lou, me and Lora was on the outs—bad outs," he says. "Been that way going on five years. She was curious, real curious, wore me out. One of them high-stepping pretty gals a man thinks is a honor to see if he can satisfy till he finds out he can't no more; they ain't enough money or time or love to keep her up, and then it's all downhill when she goes to getting old and losing her looks, her weapon. She didn't never go inside herself to find out what was there, just talked a lot about wanting to paint pictures or decorate houses, but I guess that might of turned into a weapon too."

He shifts in the chair, looks at the window, as black with darkness now as it had been with paint.

"Got to where I expected any day to find her dead—all that old Valium and vodka—but not gone," he says. "Nobody don't know this, but she threatened to kill herself that day, told me on the telephone she was going to the pond and drownd herself. How come I had them drag the pond, though I got all idees she just walked off. Or maybe drownd herself in the river back of my place. That's the kind of thing she'd a-done to get back at me, make me suffer."

"Hush yo mouth!" Louise says. "Ain't no woman gone kill herself to make somebody suffer."

"Lora would. She was crazy but she was smart. She'd want to be remembered for something on this old earth, if it wadn't nothing but dying different from everbody else around here. She hated this place, didn't never fit in, didn't want to fit in. And for a fact didn't nobody try to buddy with her—you know how come. And maybe I oughta left here a long time ago, but this is home, I got land here." He gets louder. "She wouldn't a-been no happier if I'd moved her to hell, where she could of buddied with the devil."

"You be talking bad about the dead, boy."

"I know it, Mama Lou. I get like this, I go to wanting to tell stuff." He sucks the noodles from his spoon to his mouth. "It was me much as Lora—more, I reckon. Had me another woman's what it was. How come this here's killing me." He drops his spoon into his bowl and covers his face with those old, stiff, stubby fingers that somehow still look little-boyish to Louise. Her boy. But at the same time he looks too big for her kitchen.

He peers up with pupil-less aqua eyes. Eats again. "I ain't seeing her no more, the girlfriend, if that's what you wondering, Mama Lou. Not since the day Lora went missing. Guess you know what'd happen if the law got wind of this business about the girlfriend and Lora threatening to kill herself. They'd think I done it. They'd think I killed her and done away with the body, don't you see?" He places both forearms on the table, each side of his bowl, and leans toward Louise. "I didn't kill her, Mama Lou. I swear to God above I don't know what went with her."

Louise starts to blurt out that Lora is dead, that she's in the well behind his house, dead. She aches to say it, get it over with for him and for Roper. But she doesn't and doesn't till the soup is all gone and the drunk talk turns to sober talk and old times—how tired he and Roper were that day they helped his daddy seine fish, tramping in rubber boots from the banks of the pond to the pickup with buckets full of fish—and he leaves through the same door she had steered him through an hour, two hours, before. And then she tells herself it is over anyway for Math, because his love for Lora was dead before she died.

16

It is on Tuesday evening, three weeks before the church play, that Louise's world blows up. Such a spring-like day for December, for disaster.

Following Math Taylor's visit, she had concluded that the truth wasn't all it was cracked up to be. That only heartache would result from Roper telling the truth and from Taylor telling the truth, and some things were better left to lies. That Lora Taylor should stay in that well.

That morning, with Roper gone to work and the boys at school, Louise had wrapped an early Christmas present for Roper: an oversized shoebox that once contained one of the boys' clunky shoes, now containing "the shoe," so small it rattled inside the box as she turned it this way and that, covering it with used Christmas paper kept pressed between the cushions of her couch.

Folding and taping the paper, she wondered why she hadn't thought to gift-wrap the shoe before—she was truly tired of it now—to keep from carrying it around in her apron pocket or pocketbook. Roper wouldn't have bothered the gift, couldn't care less about Christmas, but the boys probably would have. She held up the green and red holly-sprigged box to the light of the living-room window.

Maybe she should wait till after the church play, she thought, to give Roper the shoe. But he'd earned it, he'd proved himself, and she agreed with him now that he shouldn't tell Math Taylor the truth about his wife being dead. It was too close to over—all but the guilt—Taylor was too close to healed. But she would have liked to know, if it weren't too risky and damaging to both men, whether Roper would have done the right thing and told Math Taylor the truth, to set an example for the boys if not out of compassion. And she would have liked to know whether Taylor would have done the right thing and told the sheriff the truth about Lora Taylor threatening to kill herself on Halloween day.

❖ ❖ ❖

When Louise was little and living at home with Pappy and his second wife, Irene, who was young enough to be Louise's big sister, Pappy and three of his drinking buddies came rumbling up the wooded lane late one evening in a mule-drawn Hoover buggy, squatting for their knees to absorb the shock of the rubber tires' eating into the rutted dirt. Laughing and hooting, Pappy sailed over the boxy wood frame when the buggy drew level with the front porch—left hand wrapped around a fruit jar of clear bubbling shine and right hand wrapped around the head of a possum with its skint tail curled.

"Cotch hisself a possum, yes ma'am!" the men in the Hoover buggy said to Irene, waiting with her four boys in the yard for Pappy's next liquor customer. "Sho nuf, he jump right down off this here wagon and head down the ditch and cotch that old possum for yo supper."

Pappy gazed cross-eyed down at the lifeless-looking possum, whose gray ruff was stained red with blood, raised the quart jar to his pale lips and took a deep swig, then eased over to the tumbledown doorsteps and sat next to Louise and rested the hand with the possum on the step between them. Blowing, whistling, while the men and Irene and her boys headed down the woods path toward Pappy's liquor still, he spoke low to Louise without looking: "Baby-girl, see can't you help get this sonabitch to let go of Pappy's hand fore they get on back."

Louise leaned close with the curly possum tail against her bare leg, and saw that the possum's pointed teeth were pinned through the flesh between Pappy's purplish thumb and forefinger. The possum stirred, unkinking its tail like the body of a coiled snake.

Louise stood, backed. "Pappy, you ain't cotch no possum," she said, "possum cotch you."

"Ain't nobody ever know that but us if he just let go now."

❖ ❖ ❖

"Why you tell me my daddy Low Rackard, a man get kill in a sawmill muckup before I be born?" Roper has parked the Isuzu in Louise's yard for the first time—dead giveaway that something is wrong—and now struts to where she is waiting on her doorsteps.

"What you up to?" Her teeth feel lemon-sharp, ache.

"Math Taylor tell me he my brother."

"*Half* brother."

"*Half* brother, *whole* brother—who care?"

"How come him knowing all that? How come him telling all that?"

"Drunk man'll say what on his mind." Roper snorts. "Say his daddy say, 'Take care of Louise, take care of

Louise boy.' I say, 'We ain't none of his old man's mules, we ain't no pets.'"

"Wainer Taylor done take care of me. He done take care of my boy." She leans against the door frame, hugging her warped body in the silly orange velour pantsuit. "I love Wainer Taylor. He love me."

"Like you say, Mama, I belief the first but not the last." Roper slings his brown plaid overshirt from his left shoulder to the clean dirt.

"Why? Cause I be a field hand or cause I be a black woman?"

"Both."

"Well, you be whiter'n I think then."

"I ain't neither one, black or white. Am I, Mama?"

"You black, and know it. Black as me. Just yaller-skinned. Like Wainer Taylor be white and know it. Know ain't no place around here for mixing. But he love me. How come him to walk me up the courthouse sidewalk that day in that pretty flare-tail frock he buy me. Say to the world, I be proud of this woman. Weren't all to do with no voting, but a lot to do with freedom. You love somebody, you want em free. How come him to will me these bad peoples here with the land they on." She sits on the top doorstep with her elbows on her knees, scratching her burry gray head. "Sometime I think to myself Wainer Taylor must not-a love me, to saddle me with this." She waves one hand in a circle about the quarters, where televisions drone and dogs bark and people call out to one another. Drenty clothes snap on clotheslines in the sudden breeze. "A curse on me, a curse on you, now you be taking over," she adds.

"Me? What I want with this place of that crazy old man's."

"Ain't yo choice—you theirs, they yours. Cuss God." She covers her face with her long, knobby hands and cries silently.

He looks back, steps back. "I ain't feel sorry for you, Mama. I ain't feel sorry for you like I done Math Taylor these last few weeks."

She looks up, sober-eyed, but with tears streaking her dry black face. "Anybody can't feel sorry for that man can't feel sorry for the Lord Jesus nailt on the cross. All that traipsing round, looking at women's daid bodies; the law after him; peoples hoping he get sent up whether he kill nobody or not."

Roper squats, doodling in the dirt with his right pointer finger. Nonsense X marks, connecting at four points. "I tell him the truth."

Louise gasps. "That before or after he tell you?"

"After."

"To hurt him or help him?"

"Both. I be bout to tell him before."

"You hurt yo ownself, Roper Rackard."

He stands up, facing her, then gazes back at the road with listening eyes. "I gotta go on to the shurf now, Mama. To jail."

"You be out before you know it," she says. "They got ways of telling if a woman die on her own or somebody kill her."

He shrugs. "Math Taylor say come tell you what I have to tell and come on back." He stops, coughs, then adds in a strangled voice, "Tell them bad boys I say behave. Don't, they in for a whipping when I get back."

He walks off toward the Isuzu, parked for the first time in Louise's yard.

❖ ❖ ❖

From the TV Louise and the boys find out the rest of the story, the part that comes to pass after the brown sheriff's car vanishes over the hump of the railroad overpass, southbound—Roper being booked on suspicion in the Cornerville courthouse, then escorted off to the one-cell jail in the courtyard—then north of the overpass, the Taylor place with cameras panning the old homesite and the great tree collapsed on the mouth of the well.

"Man!" says Bloop. "How Roper manage that?"

"Tornado," says the round gray male reporter, as if in answer.

"Hush!" says Louise, up close to be sure she doesn't miss a word, though the TV is turned to top volume.

An autopsy will be performed at the state crime lab in Moultrie, Georgia, to determine if Rackard is guilty of murder—the reporter doesn't say or what. Until then Rackard, who is currently on probation for drug trafficking, will be held without bail, pending the outcome of the autopsy. Then an interview with Taylor, looking on as the tree trunk is sawed into sections.

"I been knowing Rackard my whole life," Taylor says to the reporter. "Ain't never knowed of him hurting nobody but his ownself."

The microphone, like some shrunken head, seems to be speaking back to Taylor: "Most people would think you'd be angry with Rackard, if in truth he did conceal your wife's body."

"I am," says Taylor and steps away as the center section of the tree trunk is forklifted and hauled from the wellsite. The microphone follows Taylor. "That's all," he says and walks toward his white pickup with the camera focused on his wrinkled neck and his thin, wet curls.

It is raining at the Taylor place on TV, but Louise and the boys can't tell that it is raining until Taylor's truck pulls away from the old homesite and his wipers start sweeping the windshield. And then they listen in amazement to the invisible rain tapping on the trailer roof.

Breakaway to a tall young woman with long blond hair, holding a blond baby on one slim hip: the young woman is crying while an older woman holds and rocks her in her arms. The camera keeps close range while another reporter retraces the sorry beginning, with Halloween day and the Taylor woman's disappearance, Rackard's working there all that time—making connections—how now the family can lay Lora Taylor to rest and get on with their lives. Then says to the young woman, dabbing at her aqua eyes with a tissue, "I guess it's a relief to finally know the whereabouts of your mother, right?"

"No," she says. "Before I could hope she was just missing, might one day turn up."

"Turn it off, Granmama," says Bloop.

Louise turns off the TV and the room quickens black, only the sound of the cold pent-up rain pecking on the trailer.

17

An uneasy stillness settles over the quarters with the cold and the mallards sweeping down from the Great Lakes to southeast Georgia. Late evenings, Louise can hear the ducks fretting, their wings whipping in the dirty-ice sky like storm gusts. Smoke billows from the shanty chimneys and yard fires, and men and women, bundled up in coats and knit hats, stand cross-armed and gaze into the braiding flames. The usual traffic sounds on the highway, dogs barking somewhere, and now and then a high-pitched shout, but something is missing: the children.

One whole week they have been down with the flu, and one whole week Louise has tended them by day, till her own pending headache, chills, and sore throat implode. Her eyes draw as if rubber bands are hooked from her eyeballs to the back of her head. Her legs are heavy as tree trunks.

She lies on the couch, watching TV, waiting for news of the autopsy and a glimpse of Roper where he is now, Roper in jail, but each day she has seen only the same handcuffed, shock-eyed Roper being led from the sheriff's car to his cell; and this evening—same picture as before—she is dozing feverishly when the latest news is delivered by the same tall woman with fixed brown hair. Something about a grand jury, Louise thinks, then finds herself staring fix-eyed at the green and blue weather map with a southward-sagging line of arrows she imagines as the mallards' wings. She gives in to aching waves of drowsiness and snuggles deeper beneath the double layer of quilts, so cold her skin feels like an ice casing for her quivering insides. No lights inside the trailer, and she sinks into the oblivion of the mallards' cry.

From time to time, Bloop or Beanie speaks to her, shakes her, but she stays still, shivering and aching, for the first time ever not caring whether they eat supper or not. Not caring whether Roper stays in jail tonight or not—*Just don't move, everybody stay put till it's over.* Little Angel comes and snuggles next to Louise and sucks her thumb. Her colorful braid beads dance before Louise's eyes. *Be still, baby, let's sleep.*

At some point during the night, Wainer comes and places his cold hand on Louise's forehead—*Been frog gigging again?*—and lifts her head and places the wet lip of a glass to her parched lips, and she drinks. He tells her he's been cleaning sand out of the well and then she sees a long rope tied about his waist and trailing over endless hillocks of sand. "I was scared to death going down in that well, gal. Carved me a ladder in them dirt walls with my pocketknife, so I could climb back out if my rope broke." Louise hears water roaring like a river and opens her eyes and Beanie is standing before her, holding a jelly glass of water. She sleeps and opens her eyes and it is light and Roper, who turns into Bloop, is saying, "Granmama, what ail you? You sick?" And it is dark behind her eyelids again and dim when she pries them open again and the mallards are fretting, their wings whipping in the dirty-ice sky like storm gusts.

❖ ❖ ❖

Pushed-back sounds of life going on: brooms whisking across bare floors and TV babble and water sluicing through pipes; Bloop and Beanie talking over whether to feed Louise soup or potted meat. "What she feed us when we be sick's what-soup." It's cold and oily on her tongue, and turns to cherry syrup, and turns to salty aspirin. Glass shattering and pots clanging and deep, dreamless sleep till one of the boys says, "Go get Lucy, tell her Granmama bout to die."

❖ ❖ ❖

Vague voices of Lucy and Sweet and children coughing. Bloop and Beanie coughing and Louise herself coughing. Silence that sounds like katydids shrieking. *Just don't move, you'll break if you move. Water pipes will freeze and then no water.*

"Don't you worry bout them water pipes, Miss Louise," says a woman. "Walleyed Willie and Boss done wrop them with rags." Low sap in winter keeps tree trunks and limbs from freezing, bursting. Louise drifts into a deep, dark sleep, trying to figure who is speaking and who is thinking, and drifts out again, as on a cloud, smelling the eye-burning odor of Vicks salve and hot tea she can taste.

❖ ❖ ❖

Late evening and Pappy is calling owls, and Louise from her trail through the woods listens and watches the soft, brown birds wing low and solitary over the sweetgums to Pappy's little black iron stove in the clearing where he solders radiators and builds liquor stills for hire. But he is not calling owls; he is feeding red corn cobs into the open flue of the stove, which is set on four bricks to generate a draft. The morning sun at his back is white. Louise's shoulder aches; she drops the sack of corn mash from her shoulder to the loam of dirt and leaves below. Her bare feet are the feet of a little girl, but her hands are the hands of a woman. She opens her right fist and finds a parchment husk with a worm larva inside, the kind found around old tobacco barns. *Which way is the lost cow?* she asks and the clear worm tips toward Pappy, whose oil-black hair is now dry white. He is squatting with a stick of lead solder; he jabs it into the dirt and pulls it out bright-shining. The sun is gone and in its place is the stick of silver solder and the red-blue blaze of the stove like a stormy sunset.

❖ ❖ ❖

Louise is riding on back of Pappy's truck with Plain Annie, and the cold wind is beating at their flared skirts. Louise can see Pappy's ball head through the back glass, but when she blinks and looks again it is the silver boxy head of a man in a white coat, who calls her Auntie and jabs her arm with something sharp that shoots a bitter taste into her mouth, like green plums. Annie with the sharp face, in Lucy's voice, corrects the doctor when he laughs and calls Louise Auntie again. Louise doesn't care. Her eyes seek out swarms of sparkly gnats, and her ears, the fretting of mallards, wings whipping the dirty-ice sky like storm gusts.

❖ ❖ ❖

Between trips to the bathroom, Louise on the couch drifts between sleeping and watching TV, not so cold or sore or sick, just coughing, confused about what's been said when and by whom: Math Taylor has confessed that his wife threatened to drown herself in their farm pond . . . play practice tonight . . . the same day she died . . . Roper Rackard is still being held . . . and Math Taylor . . . in the Swanoochee County jail . . . admitted that he had been seeing another woman, which precipitated numerous confrontations with his wife . . . at the church.

Preacher comes and prays over Louise a long time, so long that the prayer turns fuzzy and fades into a conversation of sorts between him and Lucy and Sweet about the church. As always, Louise with her mouth closed and the words sucking back from her mouth to her brain has to prompt him about the particulars, which he repeats verbatim. Amen.

Louise opens her eyes to find Roper, who turns into Beanie, sitting next to her in one of the kitchen chairs and Lucy and Sweet standing over her. Little Angel is gone.

"Go call up Little Taylor," says Louise. "Tell him I want a word with him. Y'all make yo'selfs scarce when he get here, and turn off that TV."

❖ ❖ ❖

When Louise wakes again, Taylor is there. Stepping easy through the front door like a big kid in a little kid's playhouse and letting in the last fretting of mallards and the fusing dusk. Since it is almost dark now, Louise figures Taylor had either been out when the boys called that afternoon or had been trying to decide whether to come or not. She is glad she has slept all that time between, rather than lie and worry about whether he would come or not. When she sees his slumped shoulders, that funeral face—a clean blue shirt and khaki pants—she figures he has just got the message and the message was that Louise is dying.

He pulls up a kitchen chair to the couch where she is lying and sits with his fingers shimmed between his knees. "That old flu's about whipped you, ain't it, Mama Lou?"

She coughs and spits a wad of phlegm into a tin can beside the couch. "I been through worsen the flu, boy. Hand me that wet rag there." She eyes the wadded rag on the table behind her head.

He shakes it out and wipes her ashy face, her parched lips. "I get to wipe your face this time," he says and smiles. "What they got you on, Mama Lou? What medicine?"

"Lucy and them take me to the doctor. He give me a shot and a order for some pills." She eyes the table behind her again: a brown bottle of green capsules with typing on the side, a squat blue jar of Vicks salve, aspirin, cough syrup, and a new clock with an old-paper face. The windup kind. Two orangy grade-school pictures of Bloop and Beanie standing before a fake board fence. The pictures have curled so that they stand on their own without benefit of frames.

After he finishes wiping her face, he holds the rag in his hands. "Looks like evertime I say something I open up a whole new can of worms," he says.

"That old likker talking," says Louise and turns her

face to cough into the green couch cushions she feels grown to.

Taylor shifts his broad haunches on the bird's perch of a chair, chrome legs on the brink of buckling. His blue shirt and red face are bright against the darkening backdrop of the silent room. Sickroom still, sickroom dense, save for the gray-glow TV screen and jalousie windows seeming to suck light. "Mama Lou, I'd of told Roper anyhow, drunk or sober. It was time."

"How come you to tell the law the truth about you and Miss Lora?"

"Cause I know Roper didn't kill her, ain't in him to kill nothing or nobody. Used to, we'd set out beaver traps by old fence posts in them dammed-up ditches, and Roper'd have a fit when we come up on where one had gnawed its leg off to get out of a trap."

"You think telling all that gone make em go lighter on Roper?"

"Ain't no lighter to it," says Taylor. "Way I hear it, they fixing to let him loose. Report just come in after dinner. According to the state crime lab in Moultrie, Lora's body was still in good enough shape for them to rule out it being murder. What they call 'process of elimination,' in a case like this. No lick to the head or nothing, just a few bruises—no damage to the brain. Water under the bricks where the old well'd caved in kept it cool; pecan shade overhead didn't hurt none. Course it's been cool here lately anyhow. Said if she'd been a fat woman and it summertime and her body'd been out in the open, it'd been a different story."

"What kill her then?"

"They thinking it was likely a heart attack—traces of

disease in the coronary arteries, they say. I still say it was all that old Valium and alcohol mixed, but that's just between me and you—cause of our girl, you know. Either way, ain't nobody killed Lora."

"Then how come Roper still in jail?"

"Could be, him being on probation and all, they have to go through the motions. You know how the law is. Besides, he did do away with a body; that's some kind of crime."

"I reckon you bent on telling the world he be your half brother too."

"I done told that to Roper," he says. "Anybody else wants anything told, they have to do the telling."

She rears her head, coughs, rests it on the pillow again. Too much weight to hold up, an iron head. "Me and yo daddy done go through all that. Long time ago. Ain't nobody business what we do, he tell me. Ain't nobody but the chirren what suffer, I say."

"He told me, Mama Lou. Told me to do what you say do bout all that."

"You see Roper again?"

"A little while ago."

"He overed his mad fit?"

"He ain't mad with me no more, Mama Lou. He's mad at his daddy. My daddy."

"And me?" she says.

Taylor wipes her face with the drying cloth. "Truth is, Mama Lou, I don't figger Roper's gone come home. I offered him his old job back, since he's still got that debt hanging over him, but I don't know as he's gone come to me either. Course he don't know how sick you are."

"Don't nobody tell him then." This time she turns her

face toward the familiar green couch cushions to hide her weepy eyes.

"Mama Lou," says Taylor. "Look at me, look at me."

She looks, swallows, closes her eyes.

"Mama Lou, I went through the same thing Roper's going through when my daddy told me. Me nothing but a boy then, just old enough to be worrying about what everybody in the world thought about me but me.

"Wadn't that I didn't love you, Mama Lou. It wadn't that. I just come to think of you as one of the coloreds after I got up some size. Course before that you was my mama, you know that too. Wadn't nobody I loved better'n you, unless it was my daddy.

"Till I got up some size, I didn't even know they was no difference in coloreds and whites. Except like somebody having red hair and somebody blond or black." He laughs, reaches out and strokes her arm. "Member how I used to rub Roper's head to fall asleep?"

She laughs, then cries.

"You ain't up to hearing all this right now, Mama Lou. I'm going."

He stands, then sits as she tugs his hand and holds it between both of hers. "See, I'd done come to love you before I found out," he says, "maybe that summer me and Roper wrassled that old declawed bear to get free tickets to that tent sex show, and they made me set on the white side and him on the black side. Course we was done used to that, since Roper had to get off the bus at one school and me at another one. What was we, eleven, twelve, when we wrassled that bear?"

"Wadn't old enough for no sex show," she says. "Old tent-show man oughta been whipped."

"Aw, Mama Lou," he says and laughs, "wadn't nothing to it—old gal stuffs her drawers down the drainpipe, then calls up the plumber and . . ."

"What I tell you bout talking trash like that?" she says and spanks his hand.

He spells her with his eyes, his little-boy smile. "Afterwhile, didn't nothing else matter but us, Mama Lou."

She squeezes his hand. "Roper don't have no such feelings."

"No ma'am, he don't. Maybe cause he quit tagging behind you to the big house when he was about ten and just took as fact that you was our housekeeper. Maybe I should of told him before, maybe Daddy should of . . ."

"He try."

Perfect silence while the clock on the table ticks, then: "I gotta tell you this, though, Mama Lou." He looks off then down at her again. "I didn't never tell Lora or our girl, Cindy. You know how come?"

"I know. And you do right."

"I don't know that I did right. I think I'm bout as redneck as the next fellow riding around here in a pickup truck."

"I love Wainer Taylor; he love me."

"And I'm your boy, and don't you forget that." He lowers his head. "Roper too."

She says in a high, tight voice, "Anybody tell you how Bloop and Beanie take hold and look after me while I be sick?"

18

At Lora Taylor's funeral, Saturday before Christmas on Monday, Louise takes her place at the left rear, friend-of-the-family side, of the small Baptist church where Wainer's funeral had been preached, sitting this go-round because she's too weak to stand, and just because . . . She figures she's earned the right to sit from simply having lived in Withers all her life. Among other things.

She could have sat almost anywhere she chose, actually, because out in the ten pews, friend-of-the-family side, she could count only nine people. Most of them she'd never seen before. A couple of young couples who Louise imagines are friends of Math Taylor's Cindy. One with a colicky baby, who grunts between cries.

Up front, below the cedar altar and pulpit, are a few flower arrangements: a potted purple hydrangea, a Styrofoam heart with red roses, a wreath of yellow mums and ferns, and two pots of red poinsettias.

A skinny woman in a mother-of-the-bride purple brocade dress is playing the piano. Slow, sad song.

The pews on the right side of the church are empty, awaiting the family.

Louise muffles her coughing with her handkerchief and holds her pocketbook on her lap. Then stands as the funeral director strolls up the aisle and asks everybody to stand and remain standing till the family is seated.

Holding to the pewback ahead, Louise watches as
Math Taylor in a snug navy suit and Cindy with her curly
blond baby parade up the aisle before at least a dozen
old aunt and uncle types, who might be family of Lora
Taylor. Louise can pick out only one Taylor cousin she
remembers from the old days, but Ginger—if the woman
is Ginger—looks too old, short, and thick to be Ginger,
though her fake-black hair is the same cropped, pouffy
style and her plum lipstick and rouge the same shade—
even gold hoop earrings big as bangle bracelets—as
when she used to come out to Withers with old aunts
Frieda and Sally from Valdosta to spend the day with
Cousin Wainer in the country. Ginger would talk precious to Louise and make a big fuss about her cooking.
"Sweet lil ole Louise"—loose hug—"I don't know what in
the world Cousin Wainer and Little Taylor would do
without you. I just love you for taking over after Miss
Taylor died. God'll bless you." She would dunk her own
dinner plate in the dishpan of sudsy water for Louise to
wash.

Aunt Edith and Uncle Ronald would be dead by now,
seemed half-dead then to young Louise when they used
to drive up from Florida in their long silver car and fat-
ten up for two whole days on Louise's good cooking. On
the sly, while Aunt Edith and Uncle Ronald toured the
farm on the Old Mahaffy place—the cattle would come
up late spring evenings with sooty socks and faces from
grazing the wiregrass in the woods burned off that winter—Wainer would follow Louise about the house, while
she washed dishes and clothes and floors, and shake her
arm, saying, "Law, gal, I'm sorry; law, gal, it's about time I
make an honest woman out of you." Louise would always

wonder whether he really would have if he could have, if she hadn't threatened to leave every time he offered to make an honest woman out of her.

She surprises herself by thinking now that she should have tested Wainer Taylor, should have tested the times then, but cannot imagine it and knows going public with her dishonesty would have made only Wainer Taylor more honest.

She sits down with the others on the friend-of-the-family side, as the family is seated and the preacher steps up to the pulpit and the funeral director strolls down the aisle toward the back again. But when he gets to Louise's pew, he leans down and whispers to her, "Mr. Taylor and his daughter have requested that you sit with the family," and helps her up with her pocketbook and guides her over to the family side of the church.

Not since the star hung over Bethlehem have there been so many angels, and never so many with clothes-hanger wings wrapped in gold tinsel roping.

Louise thinks that Lucy and Sweet have overdone it on the angels—six would have done nicely.

But that's all right.

And it's all right that Beanie has declined the role of either Joseph or Santa Claus (actually he had stalked off last night after supper, after Louise told the boys their daddy is getting out of jail but not coming home). Bloop is doing Joseph ("I ain't care if he never come back, we got you, Granmama, all that matter," he'd said).

This one Christmas Eve, Louise refuses to let anybody, anything—including Roper—keep her from glorying in the fact that over half the quarters have shown up at church.

From her perch on the front row, she watches the angels scratch and bump wings and cough and Bloop as Joseph balance on one knee and the other foot on the floor and the truly-pregnant Mary bat her eyes over the sun-leached doll in the cardboard box on a bed of real hay. The three wise men twist and mouth the words of "Joy to the World" while the angels sing and Ahab's boy, the shepherd, keeps time to the music by pecking on the floor with a tobacco stick. A tinfoil star rotates on cotton twine overhead.

Sweet, at the piano, is splendid in red tights and sweater, fat foot pumping the pedals. Those red spike heels rocking.

To the left of the altar is a giant longleaf pine, with wrapped presents beneath, branches decorated with construction-paper chains and cutouts of children's hands, and lights. Twinkly tiny white lights. The kind that tangle and knot and one bulb goes bad and you have to go through the entire chain, plugging each socket with a good bulb to find the problem bulb that ninety percent of the time is the last one tried. Louise figures she'll be the one to have to take down the tree and pack up the lights and clean up the pine needles later.

That's all right.

❖ ❖ ❖

Not since the star hung over Bethlehem, and never such a mangling of St. Luke's report of the Christ child's birth.

Louise faults the statue-of-a-preacher, grinning on her right, for not prompting the children better.

But it's a start. The church is full. And yesterday, at Lora Taylor's funeral, Louise had passed for an old friend, family side. Beat standing in the back thirty years ago.

When the play is over and the itchy angels have gone to their seats and the wise men have lope-walked to the rear of the church, the preacher in his tight white clerical collar steps up to the lectern.

"We be beholding to you all that come together to put on this play: Sister Sweet for playing the piano and Sister Lucy for seeing to it everbody be here for practice. And Brother Willie and Brother Boss back there for bringing us this fine tree."

Somebody at the back claps, then another.

"But most of all, and again, we have Sister Louise to thank for seeing to Christmas this year." Then to Louise in the front pew, "Sister Louise, we love you, we glad you back on your feet."

Everybody claps.

"Now most of y'all done knows Santy Claus ain't gone make it tonight"—a few groans, mock and for real, while he holds up both huge tawny hands—"so you have to put up with me this year."

Everybody laughs.

"But first," he continues, "let me get these announcements out of the way." He gazes down at a sheet of white paper on the lectern. "Next Sunday be New Year dinner on the ground, so everybody bring some good eating for the preacher."

Nobody laughs, and a few are shuffling, children whining, coughing, coughing.

"Next, Sister Louise say to tell you she be picking up

people to go register to vote at the Cornerville court-house next week. Next year be a lection year and ever-body need to put in a vote."

Behind Louise, there are a few moans, much shifting, but as far as she can tell nobody is leaving.

"Next on my list," says the preacher, "is prayer meet-ing, at seven next Wednesday evening."

"Stop running off at the mouth, fool!" Louise whispers to herself and wonders if he has heard her because he steps down from the platform in his black patent shoes and walks toward the Christmas tree.

"Now," he says, "you babies what draw names in Sunday school a while back come up and get your pres-ents when I call your name."

A few of the children squeal, stand.

"One here for . . ." The preacher holds up a thin pack-age of gold foil to the light, trying to read the name on the tag.

Suddenly, from the back of the church comes a loud banging of doors and heavy steps and a voice booming, "Ho Ho Ho, Mer-ry Christmas!"

The children shriek and laugh and cough.

Louise turns around and sees somebody in her old patched-up Santa suit with shred cotton glued to his rouged, cream-brown face and white nappy hair and black-plastic trash bags for boots and a pillow for a belly under the backward-buckling black plastic belt, even a giant-sized black plastic trash bag with real toys (a pink doll-box corner has poked through the plastic) slung over one shoulder. Trudging on up the aisle with chil-dren trailing, their eyes twinkling like the Christmas lights.

Boss and Walleyed Willie whoop. Bloop yells, "Go, Beanie!"

Somebody says, "Shh!"

Santa stops off to speak to a couple of seated nonbelievers, True-Mary for one, as he makes his way up the rackety aisle toward the front and the tree, then stops off at Louise and says, "I come home, Mama."

"Roper!"

"It's me, Mama."

"Where you get all that?" She slaps the plastic toy bag, laughing.

"Wal-Mart. Me and Taylor."